Warsaw knew that joining the rogues was wrong. Except, when his best friend begged him to help a pair of disgraced ex-councilmen, he couldn't say no. After all, he could never have the man he secretly loved. The guy was already mated. Warsaw joined the wrong side of a shifter war, and they lost.

While most consider Warsaw lucky because he wasn't sentenced to death for his crimes, he doesn't feel that way. The man he'd loved is dead, as is his best friend, both having died due to the shifter battle. Feeling empty inside, Warsaw does his job in silence, ignoring the nasty looks and slurs from others. His one joy is his little Shih Tzu, Jasmine.

When Jasmine is viciously attacked by an unknown shifter hell-bent on punishing Warsaw further, a sympathetic acquaintance introduces him to a warlock to help his dying dog. To Warsaw's shock, the warlock—Urskin Claspin—is his mate. Except, after everything that he's done in the name of love, Warsaw doesn't believe he deserves the happiness and peace a mate would surely give him. Can Warsaw figure out how to accept Fate's gift while discovering who still has it out for him?

His Traitor's Heart
Copyright © 2022 Charlie Richards
ISBN: 978-1-4874-3827-2
Cover art by Angela Waters

Published by eXtasy Books Inc

Look for us online at:
www.eXtasybooks.com

His Traitor's Heart
Shifter's Regime 12

By

Charlie Richards

DEDICATION

It doesn't matter how slow you go as long as you don't stop.
~Unknown

CHAPTER ONE

"A lot of people died because of scum like you."

Warsaw continued raking the fallen leaves from the Spanish moss trees separating the second and fifth hole of the golf course. Keeping his head bowed, he ignored the snarling voice. He'd heard it all before.

Plus, it's true.

"You should have been put to death with the others."

After the words ghosted over Warsaw's ear, he heard heavy footsteps crunching on gravel, telling him the speaker had headed away. He recognized the scent of the male as a lion shifter, but he wasn't certain which one. Damian had had plenty of friends, but the top-level enforcer had been best friends with three lion shifters. From what Warsaw had heard, the four-some had all come from the same lion pride to become enforcers for the council. Although not all of them had succeeded.

Damian.

Just thinking about the lion shifter who'd died as a result of the battle when the rogues had attacked the estate of Councilman Shane Alvaro caused Warsaw's gut to clench. His heart rate sped up. Even the hairs on his arms stood on end, and sweat beaded on his temples.

Blinking quickly, Warsaw breathed slowly and deeply. It took a moment, but he managed to regain control. Although, nothing could quite dull the ache in his heart.

Warsaw returned to raking and bagging the leaves. They'd fallen during the storm that had swept through the Savannah

1

area two days prior. After raking these leaves, Warsaw needed to head back to the storage shop, pick up the UTV with the bed, and grab the chainsaw. A limb had fallen from one of the willows. He needed to buck up what could be used for firewood and burn the remaining tailings.

At least it was no longer windy, which meant it was safe to start a fire.

The problem with raking, however, was that it was fairly mindless. It gave Warsaw's brain time to wander. As always when that happened, Warsaw thought of the past, his mistakes, and . . . Damian.

Warsaw recalled the last time he'd seen the lion shifter. It had been before he'd allowed his best friend, who was more like a brother—Kennedy—to talk him into siding with disgraced ex-councilmen who'd turned rogue. Talk about the mistake of a life-time.

He'd been at a barbeque at a fellow enforcer's home—Dane Drudeson. Damian had been laughing at something the host had said. His head had been tipped back as he laughed, a huge smile lighting up his handsome features. The man's expression had caused Warsaw's breath to catch in his throat, and arousal had surged through him.

Unfortunately, Damian had also had his arm wrapped around the waist of his Fate-given mate—a tiger shifter named Madison. The woman truly was a wonderful person. It had made hating Madison difficult, no matter how painful it was to watch them together.

While Warsaw had loved Damian from afar, he knew he could never have the man. Over time, he'd realized he needed to stop spending time with the shifter socially. He'd distanced himself from that crowd. That meant spending more time with Kennedy and others . . . who were homophobic assholes.

Yeah, I can acknowledge that now.

Warsaw had ended up deep in the closet, making do with

his hand and the occasional drunken tumble with a bar floo-zie. He'd become bitter and jaded. After several years living like that, Warsaw had lost his way—and his will to live—and when Kennedy had approached him about joining the rogues, Warsaw was embarrassed to admit that he hadn't put up much of a counter-argument.

Yeah. I fucked up.

At least I pulled my head out of my ass before flushing the rest of my life down the crapper.

While it had shocked Warsaw, he'd realized that Nkosi—a black mamba shifter—was actually a spy, helping bring down the rogue organization. Instead of reporting it to their leaders, he'd approached Nkosi in private. Warsaw had revealed that he was gay, and he'd even propositioned Nkosi to prove it.

As Warsaw recalled that, he felt his cheeks threaten to heat. The snake shifter had turned him down. The man had met his mate, although he hadn't been bonded with him at that time. If Nkosi had, it would have changed his scent, betraying his true loyalties with his smell alone.

Nkosi had helped Warsaw. He'd given him a safe place to hide until after the attack the rogues had initiated. In that same attack, Damian's mate, Madison, had been killed by a trio of lions. Damian had managed to finish the battle, but he'd died of heartache shortly after.

"Hey, asshole!"

Warsaw tensed, but he continued to rake, working on the last of the piles. As he rested the handle of the tool against the trunk of a tree, he heard someone approaching along the gravel path. Picking up a large plastic bag, Warsaw shook it out, prepping it for all the leaves he would need to stuff in-side. He spotted the black pumpkin grin on the large orange bag, and he couldn't help but smile. Warsaw decided to make certain the bag was stuffed well, making it a fantastic pump-kin for whoever decided to take it as a Halloween decoration.

Just around the corner.

"I'm talkin' to you, asshole." A tenor voice sounded behind him right before an elbow slammed into the small of his back. "Pay attention and face me, you bastard."

Warsaw bit back his natural desire to growl at the offending lion shifter — a different one than before, judging by the scent. After having been a council enforcer for nearly five decades, Warsaw struggled with obeying those his animal considered weaker.

And the wiry lion shifter Warsaw turned to peer at was definitely weaker. Staring down the three-inch height difference at Lonnie, another of Damian's buddies, he frowned at the male. Warsaw dismissed the male just as quickly.

While Warsaw was on probation for his crimes, he didn't answer to Lonnie. The man wasn't even a guard or tracker for the council. He was probably there to have a meal with Enforcer Richmond since Warsaw knew the third man of Damian's trio of best friends, Priest, was a tracker and out on assignment.

Even a disgraced ex-enforcer heard plenty of gossip. Besides, Nkosi spoke to Warsaw now more than he ever had in the past. Of course, that could have been because of Prescott, Nkosi's wood duck shifter mate. The man was as social as they came, and he always invited Warsaw to every function imaginable, whether he was the host or not.

Lonnie grabbed Warsaw's upper arm, making him jostle the rake as he attempted to fill the bag. "Hey, asshole," the belligerent lion shifter snapped. "I asked you a question."

Warsaw hadn't been bothering to listen. "Lonnie, I'm working here," he replied, barely keeping his tone in check. Rolling his shoulder, he easily broke Lonnie's grip on his arm. "I have a lot to do. Please move on."

"I asked who ya let fuck ya in order to get this cushy gig." Warsaw assumed Lonnie was repeating himself as the smaller shifter spoke and reached for him again. "Cause ya sure as hell don't deserve it. All you rogues shoulda been put down." Curling his lip, Lonnie continued, "Even that damn guinea pig shifter they picked up at the warehouse was guilty by association." He lowered his voice as he grumbled, "Can't believe they let him off without even a warning."

Warsaw knew Lonnie was referring to Miggs, a sweet guinea pig shifter who'd ended up being Enforcer Delanrue's fated mate. Miggs really had just been in the wrong place at the wrong time. He hadn't been part of their rogue group. Warsaw would have known.

Ex-councilman Paraben would have sold Miggs to the scientists in a heartbeat. He could think of several rogues who'd joined them that never made it to the fight, and it wasn't because they'd deserted like he had. Instead, Paraben's contacts had made him an offer to help fund the shifter's operation . . . in the form of buying certain rogues.

Asshole.

When Warsaw had learned of that, it'd been the impetus he'd needed to approach Nkosi and walk away. He'd given Enforcer Delanrue every bit of information he could on the scientist, Doctor Monren, and Paraben's military contact, General Saxx. While Warsaw knew the Shifter Council was working on bringing them down, he didn't know the specifics, and that was the way he liked it.

If I don't know, I can't be accused of passing information onto them if anything goes awry.

"Well?" Lonnie asked snidely. Then his eyes narrowed, and he curled his lip in a sneer. "Ya know. If you're bendin' over for some councilman or enforcer"—he reached down and grabbed his junk, jostling it—"you can bend over for me."

While Warsaw was aware that Lonnie was bisexual, he also knew that he was dating a tiger shifter named Rita.

Dick.

Disgusted by Lonnie's accusations, Warsaw glared at Lonnie. "Rita wouldn't appreciate learning about this conversation," he stated pointedly. In truth, he'd heard that Rita was a selfish, entitled bitch. How she'd ended up friends with the sweet and kind Madison, Warsaw would never know. "I'm not fucking around with anyone, Lonnie. If you used your nose, you'd already know that." If Warsaw had been intimate with anyone within the last few days, their scent would continue to cling to his skin unless he scrubbed damn well in the shower . . . multiple times. Unable to help himself, Warsaw added, "Must be why they rejected your application to become a tracker."

Warsaw knew the lion shifter had been turned down because he wasn't good enough. That had been over a decade before . . . when Warsaw had still been an enforcer in good standing.

"Why you little shit," Lonnie snarled, lunging toward him. He balled up his fist. "I'll teach you."

Pivoting to the left, Warsaw dropped the leaf bag and used the rake in his right hand to block Lonnie's punch. He blocked the next one, and the next, thinking perhaps he should have kept his mouth shut. Except, the guy really was an asshole.

Warsaw was just about to counter and lay Lonnie out when a deep voice called, "Hey." There was a distinct growl in the bass voice, and Warsaw knew who'd stumbled upon them — Enforcer Delanrue Drudeson. "That's enough, Lonnie."

Even after Delanrue's order, Lonnie still took another swing. Once again, Warsaw easily blocked the move. Lonnie telegraphed his movements worse than anyone Warsaw had fought in a long time.

Maybe there was more than one reason Lonnie hadn't gotten that tracker position.

Delanrue wrapped a beefy arm around Lonnie's torso and hauled him backward. "That's enough," he stated again, the growl much deeper, causing the hairs on Warsaw's neck to stand on end. Even his buffalo grumbled uneasily in his mind.

"When I say that's enough, I mean end it." Delanrue shoved Lonnie toward the left before crossing his thickly muscled arms over his chest. "Tell me why the fuck you were attacking Warsaw, Lonnie."

"He insulted me." Lonnie cracked his knuckles, glaring mutinously at Warsaw. "This piece o' shit rogue had it comin'."

Warsaw kept most of his attention on Lonnie, remaining ready, just in case he went against Delanrue's orders.

Would he be that stupid?

"Warsaw is no longer labeled a rogue by decree of the council," Delanrue stated, his eyes narrowing. "Now, what did Warsaw say that was an insult?"

Lonnie's cheeks turned a dark hue. From his scent, it was a mixture of rage and embarrassment.

Delanrue arched a brow, turning his attention on Warsaw.

Responding to the unspoken command, Warsaw admitted, "Lonnie insinuated that I was sleeping with someone in order to gain leniency." A fresh wave of irritation flooded Warsaw as he recalled Lonnie's words. "I told him all he had to do was use his nose, and he would know that I haven't slept with anyone." After a second of hesitation, Warsaw admitted, "Then I commented that maybe his inability to scent such things was the reason the council didn't assign him a tracker position."

Curling his lip, Lonnie growled as he advanced a step.

Lifting his left hand in a staying motion, Delanrue commented dryly, "I don't see how stating the obvious is an insult." As Lonnie's face managed to take on an even darker hue, Delanrue smirked as he focused on Warsaw. "Although, perhaps it wasn't *completely* necessary to say it."

Warsaw shrugged. "At least my words were true. Unlike Lonnie's."

Delanrue scoffed as he nodded once.

"You're both assholes," Lonnie hissed. Lifting his thumb and forefinger, he made a gun with them and pointed it at

Warsaw. After pretending to shoot Warsaw, Lonnie turned and stalked away. Warsaw's sensitive shifter hearing allowed him to catch the lion shifter's grumbled, "I'll find a way to prove it."

After Lonnie disappeared, Delanrue turned and held out his hand. That was when Warsaw realized Miggs stood several yards away. His brown eyes were wide in his pale face, and he clutched a bundle of fur against his chest.

Upon seeing that bundle, Warsaw grinned, and his troubles faded from his mind. "Jasmine." Even while Miggs ended up burrowed against Delanrue's side, he still managed to hand Warsaw's Shih Tzu to him. Holding up his beautiful girl, Warsaw stared into her warm brown eyes. "How's my pretty girl doing? Were you a good girl for Miggs?"

Warsaw often brought Jasmine with him while working lawn maintenance at the golf course. The private club and spa was a cover for the Shifter Council building. Although Warsaw didn't see the allure of the game, a number of shifters, their partners, and friends used the course often. That meant it had to be kept up. As part of his penance, Warsaw was placed on the grounds crew.

In truth, Warsaw didn't mind so much. He spent his days outside doing manual labor. It could have been far worse.

Unfortunately, Jasmine would have been an absolute terror about raking the leaves. She loved to play in the piles, making a mess. Even with her silliness, or because of it, Warsaw loved his little girl.

These days, Jasmine was his only ray of sunshine and source of joy.

When Jasmine licked Warsaw's nose, giving him a happy doggy grin, he chuckled softly. He cuddled her close and murmured nonsense. A few minutes later, he recalled who was with him and gave Delanrue a sheepish smile.

To Warsaw's surprise, the huge enforcer sported an

amused expression. There was warmth in the look as opposed to condescension. Warsaw was beginning to see just how good having Miggs as his mate was for the head interrogator, who used to be such a hard ass to anyone other than his brothers.

"I came to let you know that Rhone ended up bucking up the tree," Delanrue told him. With a shrug, he added, "He didn't know it was on your *to do* list." Pointing at the two piles of leaves he still needed to stuff into the bag, Delanrue stated, "After you're finished with these, you can be done for the day."

"Thank you," Warsaw replied, surprised and pleased. Rhone was a puma shifter and a pretty stand-up guy. "I'll have to buy him a six-pack in thanks."

"I'm sure Rhone would like that."

With most of the leaves in the bags and with his day ending early, Warsaw decided to let Jasmine have a little fun. He placed her on the ground, and she immediately bounded toward the nearest pile of leaves. Jasmine leaped into it, scattering the dry, colorful items into the air and in every direction.

Jasmine bounced on her hind legs, trying to catch the fluttering items in her jaws. Chuckling, Warsaw used his rake to cause a few more to feather through the air. With a yip, Jasmine lunged into the air once more, attacking the leaves.

Behind him, Miggs giggled, and even Delanrue chuckled softly.

Obviously spotting the second pile to the right, Jasmine streaked in that direction. She barreled through the pile, sending leaves flying. Her momentum took her through the bushes beyond the pile, and she disappeared from sight.

A second later, Jasmine's high-pitched yelp filled the air.

Warsaw dropped the rake and raced toward where Jasmine had disappeared. With a leap, he barely cleared the eight-foot-high hedge he'd ever-so-carefully manicured the day before. Landing on the other side, Warsaw froze, his breath catching in his throat.

"Jasmine," Warsaw cried, dropping to his knees beside his downed Shih Tzu. "Oh, sweetheart."

Blood poured from her side in four long gouges that looked like the work of a large predator. She whined softly, her legs twitching. Jasmine's pretty brown eyes were clouded as she stared up at him.

Tears filling his eyes, Warsaw rested his hand over Jasmine's head. He didn't know where else to touch. Her gorgeous brown fur was covered in blood.

"Oh, baby." Warsaw shook his head, disbelief flooding him.

"Shit," Delanrue rumbled. "What the hell?" The enforcer whipped off his shirt and pressed it over Jasmine's bleeding side. "Apply pressure."

On instinct, Warsaw obeyed, his heart breaking upon hearing Jasmine's whine of pain.

"Who would do this?" Miggs whispered, sounding aghast.

"I'll get help," Delanrue declared. "Stay here, Miggs."

A second later, Miggs landed on his knees beside Warsaw. "Del will get a doctor, Warsaw," Miggs murmured. He gently touched Jasmine's paw. "Hang on, Jasmine."

Jasmine whimpered once more.

"I smell cat," Warsaw whispered, anger surging through him. Unfortunately, with the heavy tinge of Jasmine's blood filling the air, too, he didn't have any hope of differentiating what kind of cat or who it could belong to.

"Lonnie?" Miggs whispered.

Warsaw shook his head, even though that had been his first thought, too. "Not him."

"Let me see," a melodious tenor called. "Lift the shirt."

To Warsaw's surprise, upon hearing the man's voice, he felt his blood heat. He snapped his attention to the right.

Watching a lithe black man, obviously in advancing years, judging by the gray at his temples and threading through his goatee, land on his knees beside Warsaw. At the same time, he placed a black satchel on the ground.

The stranger's scent hit Warsaw, and he sucked in a breath. *Mate!*

Warsaw's buffalo bellowed in his mind, eager and excited.

"Oh, fuck," Warsaw whispered, shaking his head as the man met his gaze with eyes the color of charcoal. "I-I . . . it's not possible." When the man cocked his head and narrowed his eyes, Warsaw blurted, "I don't deserve a mate."

"Hmmm," the man hummed as he arched one brow. "We'll discuss your poor response upon meeting your mate later." He turned his attention to Jasmine. "Let's save your dog first."

As an odd, surreal feeling worked through Warsaw, he nodded dumbly.

CHAPTER TWO

When Urskin Claspin had accepted Charon's invitation to tour the grounds of the Shifter Council's golf course, he certainly wouldn't have imagined his afternoon to turn out like this.

First of all, Urskin had only intended to indulge Charon's happiness at finally working outside again. The young dragon had been trapped in human form for a decade by a malicious dragon elder—Elder Gaithnos. The male had been angry that Charon had spurned his asshole son's advances.

Fortunately, being in the vicinity of his fated mate on a semi-regular basis, Dakota Drudeson—even if neither had known it due to the spell changing Charon's scent—the spell had begun to weaken. When Charon had finally been able to return to his true form for the first time, Dakota had recognized him. Head Enforcer Mycroft had reached out to Urskin, who'd removed the spell from Charon, revealing his true nature to all.

After exposing Elder Gaithnos's duplicity to the dragon king—King Leortis—the elder had fled. The last Urskin had heard, Gaithnos was still on the run. Enforcer Dakota kept Charon close, worried the elder would try something, but so far, all had been quiet on that front.

While Urskin had been complimenting Charon on his plant-pruning skills—with his magick abilities, he could feel the greenery's vibrancy and health—Dakota's eldest brother, Delanrue, had arrived. He'd asked Urskin if he had any healing spells. If Urskin hadn't seen the concern etched on the Komodo dragon shifter's face, he would have been insulted.

Of course, I know healing spells.

After confirming that he did, Urskin had followed Delanrue's urging. He'd even broken into a jog, telling him exactly how urgent the situation was. Urskin felt grateful he always carried his satchel of supplies.

As a warlock, Urskin never knew when he would need incense or an ingredient to boost his abilities.

Discovering his soon-to-be patient to be a dying dog had been more than a surprise. What had shocked him, however, was the man kneeling beside the creature. His heart had simultaneously cried out to connect with the man even as it nearly broke for him.

The shifter's aura told him many things, such as the fact that he was a buffalo shifter. The most important points, however, were the fact that this man was his familiar—the one person he could bond with, boosting his magickal abilities to heights he could never experience otherwise. The other thing his aura screamed was his grief. This man's aura was riddled with the deepest shades of orange he'd ever seen in over a hundred years.

By the gods. What has my familiar been through?

Even knowing that the tears filling the large male's eyes were for the Shih Tzu bleeding out before him, Urskin knew whatever had happened to the shifter ran much deeper. The fact that he'd blurted out that he didn't believe he deserved a mate was testament to that. Something had happened to him, and Urskin intended to figure out what.

Start with healing the dog. Figure out the rest later.

With that thought firmly fixed in mind, Urskin uttered a spell that he'd only ever used on himself. The dog's eyes immediately slid closed. Her breathing slowed and appeared to stop.

"What did you do?" his familiar roared, anguish filling his

tone along with a hint of fear. He glanced back and forth between them. His deep blue eyes widened in his lightly tanned face. "Jasmine?"

"She's not dead," Urskin assured, glancing toward Delanrue and Miggs, who'd been sitting by his familiar's side. He hoped he could get some reassurance from them. "I slowed her metabolic rate."

"Take a deep breath, Warsaw," Delanrue ordered, gripping the big blond man's shoulder. "That means Jasmine won't bleed out as swiftly."

Urskin nodded. "Exactly right."

Warsaw. My familiar's name is Warsaw.

Just because Urskin could tell what type of paranormal a person was by their aura, it didn't tell him names. In some cases, it did tell him the character of a person, though. Deep grays often denoted a person riddled with selfish decisions who cared only for himself . . . someone not to be trusted. Blues, on the other hand, meant the person was kind and helpful, with a giving attitude.

To Urskin's pleasure, he saw some beautiful medium blues mixed in with the oranges of Warsaw's aura.

To care about a dog so much, he has to have a kind heart.

With the dog—Jasmine—semi-stable, Urskin opened his satchel. "Do you know what kind of animal attacked Jasmine?" He pulled out a jaw and twisted off the cap.

"Some kind of feline," Delanrue told him.

Urskin hummed as he began sprinkling a light dusting of the green powder within on the large rake-marks causing Jasmine's flesh to gape. "Then probably no bacteria, but we'll apply this just to be on the safe side." After coating the wounds, Urskin closed the bottle and chose another. He peered at Warsaw and told him, "This will increase blood production after I seal the wounds, allowing her body to quickly regenerate what was lost."

Warsaw's brows knitted together even as he nodded once.

Urskin thought the way the massive male nibbled his bottom lip was adorable, not that he would ever tell his familiar that.

Instead, Urskin returned his attention to healing the dog. He passed the jar to Warsaw, urging him to hold it. Urskin rested his fingers on Jasmine's fur. He carefully sought out the edges of the first slice and pressed them together. As Urskin did so, he began to chant one of the first spells he'd ever learned — a flesh knitting spell.

At first, nothing happened. At least not visually.

Urskin could feel the spell taking hold, drawing on the magickal power within him. The skin on his arms goose bumped, and he continued to murmur softly, the ancient language rolling off his tongue. Even when Warsaw shifted his weight next to him, clearly concerned, Urskin didn't move.

He knew the wound was healing from the inside out, correcting the internal tearing first.

Finally, the flesh at the surface weaved back together, and the wound sealed.

Warsaw choked softly, perhaps holding in a gasp or cry. The big man lifted his free hand to his mouth, and he blinked swiftly.

For just an instant, out of the corner of his eye, Urskin noticed the sheen gleaming within Warsaw's pretty blue depths. He didn't comment on it, however. Instead, he moved to the second of the four slices and repeated the process. By the time Urskin reached the fourth slice, he could feel his energy flagging.

Jasmine had been hurt badly. Whoever had attacked her had intended to kill her. After the intensive healing he'd needed to do to save her, he knew he would need to rest.

Who the hell would kill a helpless dog just to hurt my familiar?

Anger rose within Urskin for a heartbeat, two, before he forced himself to calm once more. There was no point getting upset when he had no proper outlet for it. He knew his time for vengeance on his familiar's behalf would come.

Ending the spell, Urskin lifted his hands from Jasmine's body. He pulled a knife from inside the trench coat he wore, grateful that the moderately cool fall weather gave him leave to wear it without sticking out. Urskin had dozens of hidden pockets full of all sorts of powders, weapons, and charms within them. Even still, he felt beads of sweat forming on his forearms, chest, and face.

Dismissing his discomfort, Urskin rested the blade against his forearm.

"What are you doing?" Warsaw demanded gruffly, gripping his wrist. "Why must you make yourself bleed?"

"To mix with the powder I gave you," Urskin explained, feeling a warm rush that his familiar worried for him. The hairs on his arm lifted, and tingles traveled up his skin from where Warsaw touched him. "I'll mix it in—" Urskin glanced down. "Oh."

With a shake of his head, Urskin offered Warsaw a wry smile. "You are a distraction, my familiar," he murmured before reaching into his satchel. "Nearly forgot something sort of important."

Urskin pulled a small stone mortar and pestle from an inside pouch of his satchel. After placing the bowl on the ground before him, he rested the grinding tool beside it. Then he returned the blade to his wrist, this time holding it over the mortar.

Warsaw's eyes narrowed, but he didn't try to stop him again.

After taking a deep breath to steady himself, Urskin pressed on the blade. He slowly drew the blade across his flesh, leaving a thin line of red in its wake. He ignored the slight bite of pain as he used the thumb of his opposite hand to encourage his blood to flow, catching the drippings in the mortar bowl.

Urskin noticed the way Warsaw's nostrils flared as well as how his fingers clenched. His blue eyes seemed to darken in the fading afternoon sunlight. His lips thinned, and his attention appeared riveted to Urskin's self-inflicted injury.

As soon as Urskin began lowering the knife, Warsaw snapped out his hand. He grabbed Urskin's wrist once more. So surprised by the action, Urskin didn't react when Warsaw began bringing it toward his face.

When Warsaw stuck out his tongue and licked across his cut, Urskin gasped. "Warsaw," he whispered, shock filling him. He could feel the beginning of their connection, the bond between them forging as his magick weaved between them, weak but there. His blood rushed hot, and a wave of arousal hit him, so strong in its intensity that he actually swayed where he knelt. "Oh, gods." Urskin's voice came out rough with his sudden need. Frozen in position, he met Warsaw's gaze squarely. "You just started our bond."

Warsaw's eyes widened, and his lips parted. His shock couldn't be more obvious. His expression took on that of a deer in a vehicle's headlights. Warsaw's grip tightened on Urskin's wrist, before he snapped his hand away.

For an instant, Urskin wondered if Warsaw would flee.

After swallowing so hard his Adam's apple bobbed, Warsaw whispered, "I-I'm sorry." He scowled as he flushed a lovely red shade. "I didn't mean to."

"I don't mind, Warsaw. I was just surprised," Urskin revealed. Seeing Warsaw's continued discomfort, he recalled his familiar's earlier words and knew there was so much they needed to share with each other. "Let's finish with Jasmine." Touching Warsaw's jaw, finding it smooth beneath his fingertips, Urskin urged the buffalo shifter to meet his gaze. As he peered into his shifter's baby blues, he murmured, "Then we can take Jasmine to your suite, or an empty one, and talk as we bathe her."

Warsaw nodded slowly as he once again nibbled his bottom lip, drawing Urskin's attention to his shifter's full mouth.

Damn. That move is going to be the death of me.

Urskin yanked his focus away from Warsaw's delectable lips. Placing the knife on the ground, he took the bottle from his shifter's unresisting fingers. He unscrewed the cap, then sprinkled some of the blue powder into the mortar bowl. After replacing the cap, Urskin set the small bottle aside and picked up the pestle.

With long-practiced movements, Urskin mixed the powder into his blood. Within a minute, a thick red paste filled the bowl. He placed the pestle on the grass near the knife, then held the bowl out to Warsaw.

Warsaw hesitated before taking the bowl, a look of confusion knitting his brows.

"I'm going to lift the suspension spell, Warsaw," Urskin told his familiar. "Jasmine may have some lingering pain, be a little disoriented, and she'll be sleepy from blood loss. I figure it would be best for you to do this."

"What do I do?" Warsaw asked, looking from the bowl's contents to his dog and back to Urskin.

Urskin smiled as he explained, "Grip the underside of Jasmine's jaw with one hand." He pointed where he indicated. "Ease your thumb into the corner of her mouth to encourage her to open." Indicating the mortar bowl, Urskin told him, "Dip a finger into the paste and coat the back of her tongue with it. That'll encourage her to swallow."

As Warsaw nodded, he placed the bowl near Jasmine's head while cupping her jaw with his other hand. He dipped his index finger into the paste. After a second, Warsaw brought it to his nose and sniffed it.

"It won't hurt her," Urskin assured him. "Only help."

To Urskin's surprise, and a little amusement, Warsaw stuck his finger into his mouth, licking the paste from his finger. The big shifter's eyes widened, and he hummed softly.

He even went so far as to dab his finger into the paste once more and steal another bite.

The fact that Warsaw obviously loved his flavor so much caused Urskin's blood to heat in his veins. Despite the circumstances, arousal thrummed within him. He felt his mouth water with an answering desire as his attention snagged on Warsaw's pulse point.

"Uh, guys?" Dakota muttered, revealing that he and Charon must have followed after him and Delanrue. "Not that that isn't weirdly hot and all." Dakota snickered. "But isn't that for Jasmine?"

"Shit," Warsaw mumbled, his cheeks darkening a little. "Sorry."

Urskin scoffed, admitting, "That was so hot." Then he turned his attention to Jasmine. "Time to lift this spell. Get ready."

Resting his palm on the small dog's side, Urskin quietly uttered a counter-spell he never thought he would need.

CHAPTER THREE

"Report?"

Warsaw jerked his attention from where he petted the soft fur on top of Jasmine's head. Spotting Head Enforcer Mycroft standing next to Delanrue, unease slithered through him. His gut clenched, and he worried the head enforcer would blame him.

Obviously catching on to Warsaw's concern, Delanrue leveled a serious look upon him. "Relax, Warsaw. I called Mycroft." He turned and answered his boss. "A cat shifter attacked Jasmine while she was playing in the leaves." His hazel eyes narrowed, blazing dark with anger. "There's no reason for such a callous act, even if Jasmine could have somehow been a danger, which we all know she isn't."

Everyone knew that Jasmine was a friendly dog. Warsaw had taken in the little Shih Tzu as a pup six years prior. The animal had been raised around shifters and had never been antagonistic toward them. She also had never feared them, either.

And everyone knows she's mine. She was hurt because of me.

"Whatever you're thinking about, Warsaw, cut it out," Mycroft ordered, scowling at him. Just as quickly, he turned his attention to the lithe, older-looking black man seated next to Warsaw. "How's she doing, Urskin?"

"Although Jasmine's in dire need of a bath, she'll make a full recovery," the warlock—Urskin—declared with a smile.

Warsaw noticed Urskin had pulled a rag and corked bottle from somewhere—probably his satchel—and he appeared to be cleaning his tools. As the man — *my mate* — rinsed out the last of the paste from his mortar bowl, Warsaw found his mouth watering anew.

Gods, that blood mix tastes so fucking fantastic. I could've eaten the whole bowl.

Even after several minutes, as well as the worry of having Mycroft arrive, Warsaw remained hard as nails. His cock throbbed in a way he'd never before experienced. His balls felt full and heavy, and he longed to find relief.

Preferably with my mate.

Shit. I don't deserve a mate. What was Fate thinking?

Nibbling his bottom lip, Warsaw cast a quick glance Urskin's way. The dark-skinned male cut a fine figure, even with most of his body hidden behind the trench coat he wore. His shoulders were lean, his frame lithe, and his neck was long.

Warsaw's mouth watered with his desire to lick and nip along the tendons of the man's long neck. His dark skin called for him to do his best to mark it with his mouth and teeth. His claiming mark would look absolutely fantastic on —

Damn it. What am I thinking?

Right. With my dick. Because I've actually already started the bonding process.

Fuck! What am I going to do? He doesn't deserve a jaded asshole like me.

"Hey. Hey." Urskin's warm, long-fingered hand cradled Warsaw's jaw, yanking him out of his thoughts. Tipping his chin up, Warsaw peered into eyes as black as night. "Your thoughts are spiraling, my familiar," the man murmured, his tenor voice full of kindness and his expression understanding. "Whatever past has caused you such sadness, we'll get through this." As Urskin curved his lips into a small smile, his eyes crinkled a little at the corners into crow's feet, betraying the man's age. "I'm over three hundred years old, Warsaw. I never thought to meet my familiar, but I'll be damned if I let whoever is after you come between us now." Then Urskin's expression sobered. "And whatever clouds your aura with so much sorrow, we'll work through it. I want to see you happy again."

"My aura?" Warsaw frowned, confusing filling him. "How do you know I have sorrows?"

Warsaw didn't think that question came out quite right, but Urskin seemed to understand.

"As I said, Warsaw," Urskin replied, his black eyes holding a surprising amount of warmth. "I'm over three hundred years old. I've had a long time to learn and perfect my abilities." Tracing the forefingers of his right hand along Warsaw's jaw, sending tingles in their wake and making it difficult to concentrate, Urskin told him, "I've developed the ability to see the aura of a person's psyche. It tells me if someone is a human. If they're a paranormal, what kind." As he spoke, his focus slid down, obviously following where he touched. "It also allows me to see a little of their emotional state. If they're happy or joyful. Filled with hate or the desire for revenge." Returning his attention to Warsaw's eyes, Urskin murmured, "Or even if they're filled with sadness or grief." Urskin leaned forward and nuzzled his goateed jaw against Warsaw's own as he whispered into his ear, "I don't know what happened to you, my familiar, but I wish to help you through it."

A shiver worked down Warsaw's spine. His grief and guilt welled through him, finally making a dent in his arousal. He turned his head and focused on Jasmine, no longer able to meet his mate's eyes. Warsaw couldn't handle the compassion he spotted within those dark depths. He didn't deserve it.

"I'm glad you were on hand to help, Urskin," Mycroft stated, cutting into their moment. "What do you wish for your services?"

Probably for the best. I don't know how to respond to this man. I – Wait.

"Cost for your services?" Warsaw repeated softly, jerking

his attention back to Urskin. "Oh. Of course." He should have realized that before. Urskin wasn't a shifter, and he certainly wasn't one of the doctors on the Shifter Council's payroll, who treated anyone who needed aid. "You need to be paid."

With a scoff, Urskin shook his head. "No, I don't." He lowered his right hand to Warsaw's shoulder while waving his left to indicate him. He peered up at Mycroft. "To use shifter terms, Warsaw is my mate. While I'm basically human, I would still do anything to help him."

"Your mate?" Mycroft's brows shot up, nearly hiding beneath his red hair. "How's that work with a warlock?" His green eyes narrowed. "Warlock's have . . . mates?"

Urskin skimmed his hand down Warsaw's arm until he threaded their fingers together. "No, not in the way you refer to," he replied, although his attention returned to Warsaw, holding his gaze. "Warlocks and witches have something called a familiar. Our magick guides us, allowing us to recognize that person."

For the first time in his life, Warsaw found himself holding hands with another man. His palm tingled, and zings traveled through his arm. He felt a shiver work up his spine. Even a warmth settled in his gut, causing it to churn in an odd yet pleasant way.

Um, weird.

"So, could a human be your familiar?" Miggs asked curiously. "How would that work if you're both human?"

Urskin turned his attention away from Warsaw, and he felt his buffalo grumble in his mind. Warsaw agreed. He would have preferred to have his mate's attention remain on him, too.

Shit. I already think of him as my mate. Could I bond with him even though I may never be able to love him?

After loving Damian for more years than Warsaw could remember, and the lion shifter wasn't even his mate, Warsaw couldn't imagine finding room in his heart for another. Except, he'd seen plenty of couples mate for convenience or for mutual benefit. Perhaps that was what he could share with his mate.

I'd just need to be upfront about it with him.

"Yes, Miggs." Urskin smiled at Miggs. "A warlock or witch bonds with their familiar through their magick." Returning his attention to Warsaw, Urskin held his gaze as he rumbled softly, "Our magick feels almost like a living entity within us. I figure it's similar to how you feel with your animal half." Then Urskin winked before smirking at him. "Except we can't turn into an animal."

"S-So even if I was a human, you'd still want me?" Warsaw began slowly, trying to wrap his brain around that. Then he scoffed and rolled his eyes. "Gods, and now I sound like one. Of course, you would." Meeting Urskin's gaze, Warsaw hazarded, "Because your magick is like my shifter instinct to care for and please you."

Urskin froze for a few seconds. After a quick sweep of the area and who was around—and obviously listening raptly—he nodded slowly. "There are some differences," he admitted, lowering his voice. His scent took on a hint of unease. "But we don't traditionally explain them outside of our partner."

Mycroft's slow nod, coupled with his smirk, caught Warsaw's attention. "Trade secrets?"

"Something like that," Urskin admitted.

"Soooo, you have the ability to put someone into some kind of . . . trance?" Mycroft asked. After waving toward Jasmine, who was nuzzling sleepily into Warsaw's hand where he massaged her ears, he crossed his arms over his head. "Or deep sleep?"

"Technically, yes," Urskin responded slowly, perhaps choosing his words carefully. "I know a spell which will slow down the body's metabolic rate, giving it a chance to heal naturally from some pretty serious injuries."

"But it also leaves someone vulnerable," Delanrue pointed out. With one arm wrapped around Miggs protectively, he asked, "Have you ever cast it on someone as an offensive spell?"

Urskin inhaled deeply, then let it out steadily. "It would be unethical for me to do it to a sentient being without their permission," he stated, holding Delanrue's gaze. "So, no. I've never cast it on another before, but considering Jasmine is a dog and it was the only way to save her" —he pointed at Delanrue, then Warsaw—"by your request as well as the request of her owner, I chose to utilize it." After another second of hesitation, Urskin added, "It was the only way I could think of to buy the time necessary to save her life."

"If you don't use it on others," Miggs cut in, confusion filling his voice. "Who do you use it on?"

Urskin chuckled softly. "I've used it on myself a number of times over the centuries." With a wry smile curving his full lips, he stated, "Not every paranormal is happy when they realize I'm a warlock, and I've been gravely injured on several occasions." With a grimace, Urskin admitted, "I would find a secluded place where I knew it would be okay to hole up for a while, then cast a glamour spell so no one could stumble across me, and bespell myself." After another second, he told them, "Depending on the extent of the injuries, I would sleep anywhere between two weeks and two months before waking naturally."

"Huh." Dakota cocked his head. "So it's sorta like putting yourself into a coma."

Humming, Urskin nodded. "Sort of." Then he winced and shook his head. "But not really."

Dakota barked a laugh. "Clear as mud, man."

Urskin just shrugged, his smile enigmatic.

"I'm going to track down Lonnie," Delanrue stated, his hazel eyes narrowing. His expression turned thoughtful.

Grimacing, Warsaw admitted, "He'd just attacked me, so his scent was fresh in my nose. It wasn't him."

"True." Delanrue's smile turned predatory. "But he was just here, so maybe he saw something." With Miggs in his arms, he somehow still managed to crack his knuckles. "Plus, it'll be fun to question him."

Frowning, Mycroft let out a deep sigh. "Why did Lonnie attack you, Warsaw?"

Delanrue explained, which Warsaw appreciated. Urskin had begun massaging the palm of his hand with his thumb, and the tingles it sent up his arm caused his mouth to go dry. He was having a hard time getting enough moisture into his throat as his arousal thrummed within him.

"Mycroft?" Urskin spoke up. "Is there somewhere we can take Jasmine to wash and dry her?"

Warsaw cleared his throat, finally finding his tongue. "I have an assigned suite here." He felt his cheeks heat as he admitted, "It's not as nice as when I was an enforcer, but it still has a tub."

Just not a big jetted one like my old suite. Warsaw cut a side-eyed look Urskin's way and swept his gaze over the lean black man. *Too bad, too. Because it would have been fun to enjoy with Urskin.*

"How about I take care of washing Jasmine?" Miggs offered. A sly smile curved his lips as he sniffed the air pointedly. "Considering the pheromones you're both pumping out, Warsaw, you really think you could make it through a whole washing and drying session?"

"That's a good idea." Dakota grinned broadly as he waggled his eyebrows. "You wouldn't want to damage anything important." He glanced at Warsaw's crotch before meeting his gaze again. "And that looks painful, man. Charon and I'll help Miggs while Del does his thing with Lonnie." Issuing a low chuckle, Dakota continued, "You and Urskin can head to your quarters and —" He finished by whistling meaningfully and waggling his eyebrows.

While Warsaw had never been a prude, he'd never openly discussed sex with anyone before. Well, that was mainly because he didn't want to talk about a woman's bits any more than he had to. On top of that, Warsaw had been so far in the closet for so long that he'd never had the chance — or the guts — to talk about man-sex.

Just something else to discuss with Urskin.

"Okay," Warsaw agreed, slipping his hand free of Urskin's. "But I wanna carry Jasmine to the compound." As he leaned forward and eased his still lethargic girl into his arms, he admitted, "I don't wanna be parted with her just yet."

"Understandable, man," Dakota replied, patting him on the shoulder. "Let's get moving."

Climbing to his feet, Warsaw winced as his jeans bit into his dick. The guys were right. He didn't think he would make it through bathing Jasmine without blowing his load.

Gods, how embarrassing that would be.

"I'll finish with this last bag real quick," Charon stated, pausing where Warsaw had been working. He pecked a kiss to Dakota's lips. "Then I'll meet you at Miggs's suite."

Dakota hesitated, then nodded. "See you soon," he murmured before grabbing Charon and laying a much deeper kiss on his lips.

Warsaw felt his cheeks heat as he gave in to Urskin's hand on his lower back. He wondered if he would ever be that comfortable with his mate to kiss openly.

As Warsaw trooped with the others toward the Shifter Council compound, he did his best not to feel guilty about leaving his work to another.

Urskin's hand remaining on his back certainly helped to distract him.

CHAPTER FOUR

Urskin watched Warsaw open the door by placing his thumb on the scanner. While he didn't have a paranormal's sense of smell, he could still tell that the large buffalo shifter was nervous. His familiar's shoulders were tight, and he kept casting furtive, sideways glances at him.

While Urskin knew that Warsaw was a shifter, so he would be instinct-driven to couple and complete their bond, he'd seen the way the man had reluctantly handed over his sleepy, blood-coated dog at Miggs's doorway. The shifter hadn't wanted to let the little beast go. It had been on the tip of Urskin's tongue to offer to wait, to help him wash the dog—as he had before—but then Warsaw had given Jasmine to the guinea pig shifter before reaching down and adjusting himself.

Seeing the massive bulge behind Warsaw's fly, Urskin had felt his own few seconds of trepidation. He knew that, for their first round at least, he would be the one receiving. Urskin couldn't recall how many years it had been since he'd taken a cock.

Over two centuries, perhaps.

For my familiar, I will.

Besides, Urskin knew after three centuries, he was skilled at the art of love-making. He would show Warsaw the joys of having his prostate stroked and played with. Urskin intended to teach his familiar the pleasures of switching things up in the bedroom.

Warsaw opened his door and led the way inside. Stopping

28

a few steps inside, he indicated the space. "It's not much," he mumbled. "Not like what I used to have here, but it's home for me for the next six months."

Urskin followed Warsaw into the suite, glancing around at the space. While it was nicely appointed, it reminded him of a large hotel room with a small kitchen efficiency. He spotted the bedroom through one open door and the bathroom through another. The living space sported a reclining chair and a love seat positioned around a gas fireplace with a TV above it.

Unable to contain his curiosity, Urskin asked, "What do you mean, for the next six months?" He focused his attention on Warsaw as he closed the door behind him. "Are you looking to buy a house around here?"

That might end up causing Urskin an issue because he traveled extensively. As a warlock, he would occasionally have visions of the future. Sometimes, he would feel compelled to seek out the location of his visions in order to stop or change the events. On top of that, Urskin made his living by selling his services.

Which is how I came to be in this area . . . by helping Charon.

"I'm a disgraced ex-enforcer, Urskin," Warsaw told him. His brows furrowed as his expression turned troubled. Warsaw moved to the sofa, but he paused beside it instead of sitting. As he adjusted himself, he muttered, "I chose to side with the ex-councilmen who went rogue." His cheeks took on a distinctively dark hue, and he rubbed the back of his neck as he stared at the blank fireplace. "I, uh, had some things going on in my head and didn't see a future for myself." With a wince, he admitted, "Still a little messed in the head, but I'm working on it."

Urskin's concern grew the more Warsaw spoke. "You are my familiar," he began slowly, moving toward him. He tipped his head back so he could peer into the eyes of the large shifter, who had four inches on Urskin's own six-foot height.

"I'd be more than happy to listen to whatever you feel comfortable sharing with me. Whatever's troubling you, I wish to help."

Warsaw lifted his attention from the fireplace to meet his gaze for a few seconds before his focus slid away again. He lifted a large hand and rubbed it over his scalp. Running that same hand down his face, he mumbled something Urskin didn't catch.

"I'm sorry, Warsaw." Urskin gripped Warsaw's hand in a light hold, pleased when the man snapped his attention back to him. "I didn't catch that."

Urskin did his best to ignore the way the hairs on the back of his arm lifted in response to touching Warsaw. He knew he needed his big brain engaged as he focused on the shifter. Taking care of his familiar's problems was more important than the randy state of his dick.

But, gods, it's hard. Can't remember when I've been so aroused . . . and all I've done is hold his hand.

"Uh, maybe later," Warsaw muttered a little louder. "I, uh—" He swallowed hard once more before a low growl erupted from him.

Sensing Warsaw's frustration, Urskin massaged the man's hand, hoping to soothe him. "Whatever it is. I'd like to help," he offered.

Warsaw grumbled, "I'm almost a hundred fifty years old, and I don't know how to ask for what I need."

Urskin cocked his head as he narrowed his eyes just a little. "Just blurt it out," he encouraged. "Whatever you need, I'd like to help."

"I don't wanna talk," Warsaw told him, his deep voice turning gruff. "Never been so hard before. Must be because you're my mate. Can't think of anything else." A muscle flexed in his jaw for a few seconds. Then he snarled, "How do men fuck?"

Urskin opened his mouth, then shut it just as quickly. His

blood heated in his veins, warming him from the inside out. His dick twitched behind the fly of his jeans.

"If we fuck, we *will* bond," Urskin warned when he finally managed to get his brain sort of online. There was no way in hell Urskin would be able to control his magick enough to stop it, and he didn't want to even try. "Are you ready for that?"

Pulling his hand away, Warsaw thrust it through his short blond hair once more. A worried expression creased his brows. His blue eyes took on a glazed look.

A second later, Warsaw blinked. "Yeah," he rumbled, focusing on Urskin. "Yeah, I get that." He cleared his throat, looking damn uncomfortable, before saying, "Uh, you know I don't love you, right?"

Urskin felt his brows lift, and unable to help himself, he barked a laugh. Upon seeing Warsaw's brows draw together, Urskin grinned. He shook his head as he pulled himself together.

"Uh . . ."

Upon hearing Warsaw's discomfited mutter, Urskin found his tongue. "Sorry." He couldn't help but smirk as he stared up at his familiar. "Just because I'm human doesn't mean I have that hang-up," Urskin explained. With a shrug, he reminded the man, "I'm over three hundred years old, Warsaw. I've been around the block more than once." Seeing his shifter continue to stare at him with uncertainty and concern in his eyes, Urskin told him, "I've been in love with a few people over the centuries." He squeezed Warsaw's hand. "I've heard many paranormals wax poetic over finding their fated mate and falling in love at first sight." Shaking his head, Urskin smiled at Warsaw. "I can admit to lust at first sight, but not love. No one can promise love." He squeezed his shifter's large hand as he told him, "What I can promise is to do my best by you as we learn to navigate a life together."

Warsaw stared at him for a long moment, and Urskin wondered what was going on behind the man's pale blue eyes. Finally, the big shifter nodded once. His brows were furrowed, and he glanced away, only to pin his attention back on Urskin.

"There's too much going on in my head," Warsaw rumbled on a sigh. After licking his lips, which drew Urskin's attention, he stated, "I accept what you're offering, and I'll offer you the same." Warsaw hesitated, his grip tightening on Urskin's hand. "Companionship as we figure out a life together."

Urskin smiled up at Warsaw. "I accept, as well."

While Urskin felt a little unsettled by the fact that they were talking about bonding their lives as if it was a business transaction, he would take it. After all, he knew he needed the man before him, whether he knew him or not. His magick sizzled under his skin in a way he hadn't experienced since he'd first learned to sense and control it.

I'll figure out all the particulars later. First . . . getting this man horizontal.

"You asked how men fuck." Urskin indicated the doorway where he could see the edge of the bed. "Can we take this into the bedroom?"

A muscle flexed in Warsaw's jaw for just an instant, betraying his unease. Then he jerked a single nod before turning toward the indicated bedroom. He tightened his grip on Urskin and led the way into the other room.

Warsaw stopped at the foot of the king-sized bed. After another nervous-looking glance at Urskin, he focused on the far wall. His cheeks took on a pinkish hue as he cleared his throat.

Urskin knew he would have to take the lead, even though he was sure he would end up as the bottom.

This time around, anyway.

"As a shifter, I assume you're not body shy," Urskin began, touching the hem of the large male's polo shirt. "Would you like me to strip you? Or do you want to do it yourself?"

With how nervous Warsaw appeared, Urskin wanted to be certain to get permission for everything.

"Uh, I-I'll undress," Warsaw rumbled, turning away from him.

Urskin left Warsaw to it. He understood that just because Warsaw's shifter instincts were driving him to bond, it didn't mean he was completely comfortable with everything it entailed. Urskin would do what he could to help his familiar.

"Do you have a favorite type of lube that you use to jack off?" Urskin asked bluntly as he placed his satchel on a chair near the side of the bed. "If you don't, I have cream in my bag."

It wasn't the most ideal choice, but it would work well enough for their first round.

"I-I have lube," Warsaw muttered without turning to face him. He dropped his polo shirt on the floor before crossing to the left-hand-side nightstand. "Uh, it warms."

As Warsaw pulled it out and dropped it on the bed, he wouldn't meet Urskin's gaze. Instead, he fiddled with the button on his jeans. He glanced from the lube to the far wall and back again.

"I enjoy that kind as well," Urskin told Warsaw, hoping the admission would help him relax. When he saw his familiar nod and begin popping the button on his jeans, Urskin murmured in warning, "I'm going to strip now."

Warsaw's head snapped up. Pinning Urskin with a wide-eyed look, he stared at him with parted lips. His nostrils flared, and he stood frozen.

Urskin refused to preen under the huge man's scrutiny. Instead, he did as he'd stated. He eased his trench coat from his shoulders and draped it over the back of the chair. Then Urskin unbuttoned the top two buttons on his short-sleeved button-down before tugging that over his head and off. Urskin folded that fabric in half, too, and draped it over his coat.

Facing Warsaw, Urskin spotted the way the man's nostrils flared and how his eyes widened just a smidge. His soon-to-be lover raked his gaze over Urskin's bare torso, and his body warmed from that look alone. He appreciated that Warsaw obviously liked what he saw.

While Urskin knew he was still in good shape, he couldn't hide his age. Bits of gray had infiltrated his hair, goatee, and chest hair over half a century before. While his stomach remained flat, he no longer sported the six-pack of his youth.

From the glow filling Warsaw's blue eyes coupled with the way his chest heaved faintly, Urskin knew his familiar didn't mind one little bit.

Sweeping his attention over Warsaw's massive torso, Urskin couldn't help but let out a soft, appreciative growl. His shifter sported broad shoulders with a thickly muscled torso and limbs. His abdominals were clearly defined, and if Urskin didn't miss his guess, he actually sported an eight-pack. Under his gaze, Warsaw's abdominals fluttered, and Urskin spotted the vee that disappeared beneath the fabric, causing his mouth to water with a desire to trace those lines.

"You're looking at me like you want to eat me."

Urskin snapped his attention back to Warsaw's face. Upon seeing the way he stared at him with wide eyes, he smiled at the shifter. "I look forward to licking every inch of your body, Warsaw," he admitted, keeping his smile warm. Urskin didn't want to scare his inexperienced shifter, after all. With a wink, Urskin knelt before Warsaw. "May I unlace your boots for you?"

"Um, okay."

Urskin made quick work of untying Warsaw's heavy work boots. Instead of trying to help him out of them, he eased onto the chair and toed off his own shoes. Urskin followed that up with removing his socks.

When Urskin looked up, he nearly swallowed his tongue. He couldn't help the way his eyes widened as he took in the expanse of smooth pale skin before him.

Warsaw stood before him in the buff. He had the faintest smattering of hair on his limbs and chest, which seemed to accentuate his thick muscles. His nipples were beaded, standing proudly from his tan areoles.

Now, if only Warsaw wasn't trying to hide his gorgeous erection.

The sexy shifter rubbed the back of his neck with his right hand. His left hand hovered over his groin. Even with his large hand, there was no way the man could completely hide his cock. There was just too much of it.

Urskin's mouth watered, and he forced himself to slide his gaze up Warsaw's chest to meet his gaze. "You are a stunning man, Warsaw."

When Warsaw opened his mouth, then closed it again, Urskin didn't make the man try to come up with something. Instead, he rose to his feet and undid the fly of his jeans. He pushed down the fabric, taking his briefs with them. Bending, Urskin eased them down and off before straightening once more and piling the items onto the chair he'd vacated.

Hearing Warsaw's soft inhale, followed by a quiet groan, Urskin turned and met the shifter's gaze. He didn't try to hide his hard cock, and while he didn't sport anywhere near the size of his familiar's massive tool, his erection was in good proportion to his body. Urskin appreciated the way Warsaw licked his lips, heat filling his eyes, nearly beating out the uncertainty.

Urskin eased a step forward, lifting a hand. "Will you get comfortable on the bed, Warsaw?" He could practically see the shifter vibrate with tension. "Let's start with something simple."

"Simple?" Warsaw asked, his voice husky and deep.

Nodding, Urskin touched Warsaw's upper arm. "Lie down and relax, Warsaw." He gently urged him onto the mattress.

"Trust me."

Chapter Five

Trust me.

Warsaw's heart rate sped up at those words. The last person he'd trusted had led him down the wrong path. Admittedly, Warsaw hadn't tried to counter Kennedy very hard.

I just hadn't cared.

But this is my mate.

Gods, Fate sent me my mate.

Warsaw was still struggling to wrap his brain around that fact. In no way did he think he deserved his fated mate. Still, he wasn't stupid enough to attempt to reject him.

And gods, my mate is a man.

"Warsaw?"

Hearing Urskin's soft question in that one word, Warsaw yanked his attention back to where it should be. For the first time in his life, he had a naked, willing man in his bedroom. Also for the first time, Warsaw knew that no one in his life would give him shit if they found out his lover's gender.

They'll give me shit for plenty of reasons, but this won't be one of them.

"Um, I'm nervous," Warsaw blurted out when he felt Urskin squeeze his upper arm again. He forced his feet to move and his mouth shut. "Uh, sorry."

Warsaw climbed onto the bed. Once he was there, he didn't know what to do with himself. He settled on his ass with his back to the headboard. Bending one knee, Warsaw rested his forearm on it, unable to help how shy he felt.

To Warsaw's relief, Urskin didn't comment on it. Instead,

Warsaw watched with bated breath, his gaze roving over the black man's beautiful body. His fingers actually twitched with his desire to glide his palms over the man's smooth flesh.

Urskin settled onto the bed beside his hip, resting on his knees. Slowly, he reached for him. His warm hand landed on Warsaw's shoulder.

Warsaw could see the questions in Urskin's eyes. Knowing he had to do something to reassure the older man, he blew out a harsh breath. Plus, Warsaw needed to get himself together enough to be able to do something about his aching shaft. The throb in his dick was making it damn difficult to think.

"I-I'm sorry," Warsaw murmured, clenching and relaxing his hands. "I, uh, I d-don't know what to do."

"Just try to relax, Warsaw," Urskin encouraged. "Lie back, and let me help take the edge off for both of us."

Planting his palms on the mattress, Warsaw did as Urskin bid. He slid down the comforter and stretched out, reclining on the fabric. As he stared up at Urskin, even his nerves didn't cause him to soften. Instead, as the other man sprawled out beside him, Warsaw felt his dick twitch, and a throb went through his groin, his balls uncomfortable.

When Urskin rested his palm on Warsaw's chest, he felt his breath catch in his throat. Tingles erupted across his skin, and his nipples beaded. He felt the hairs on his arms stand on end.

Warsaw couldn't help himself. With his need to touch driving him, he reached for Urskin. Hot desire burned within him. Warsaw shuddered with need as his palms met the flesh of Urskin's arms. His mate's muscles were firm under the man's warm skin.

Giving in to his basest of instincts, Warsaw yanked Urskin toward him. He felt his mouth water as he drew the man closer, eyeing the stretch of smooth dark flesh where his neck met his shoulder. His teeth ached as he fought back his desire to allow his canines to extend.

When Warsaw's unexpected move caused Urskin's body to crash into his own, he hissed with pleasure. The sizzles caused by the male's chest pressing against his own yanked a moan from his throat. Needing more, Warsaw wrapped a leg around Urskin's upper legs. With an arch of his body and a twist of his hips, Warsaw rolled them.

A second later, Warsaw was staring down at Urskin. He peered into the black man's dark eyes. As he took in the lust filling the warlock's features, along with scenting it rolling from him, Warsaw felt a fresh wash of need surge through him.

Then, for the first time in his life, Warsaw felt another man's hard cock press against his own. A harsh shudder worked through him. His blood fired through him with blissful intensity.

"Urskin." Warsaw hissed the other man's name as he froze, goose bumps erupting on his groin and thighs. His balls threatened to unload just from that single press. "Oh, gods."

"Don't fight it, Warsaw," Urskin encouraged, massaging his neck with one hand while gliding his second down his spine. "Never deny your need, my familiar."

Warsaw shivered under Urskin's petting. Shudders racked him. Even his toes curled.

Issuing a gruff roar, Warsaw gave in. His balls tightened, and his orgasm crashed through him. His senses sang as he flew on the exquisite wings of his release.

With his blood ringing in his ears, Warsaw couldn't stop his canines from extending. His bull bellowed in his mind, urging him on. Dipping his head, Warsaw sank his teeth deep into Urskin's flesh, biting where his neck met his shoulder.

As soon as Urskin's blood hit Warsaw's taste buds, he moaned deeply. He quickly swallowed before sucking for more. The oddly sweet, iron-rich fluid flowed across his tongue, and he groaned once again.

Warsaw wasn't certain how long he lost himself in the sweet bliss of his release and the taste of his mate. Absently, he registered the hard jerk of the strong, lean frame beneath him. Finally, Warsaw noted the soothing, petting strokes caressing his back.

Gaining control of himself, Warsaw eased his teeth from Urskin's neck. He focused on licking the bite closed that he'd left on the dark man's neck. To his relief, Warsaw heard the warlock hum softly.

Finding himself unable to meet Urskin's gaze, Warsaw rested his forehead on the man's collarbone. He panted softly, tingles still zinging through his system. From the corner of his eye, Warsaw stared at his claiming bite.

Even as Warsaw's buffalo rumbled with satisfaction at the sight, he felt his dick twitch. The continued ache surprised him. He'd heard that shifters who met their fated mate had an increased sex drive, but he hadn't thought it would feel so . . . uncomfortable.

After getting off, Warsaw thought he would get a few minutes of relief before needing another round.

"Hey, Warsaw," Urskin crooned into his ear. "Are you okay?"

Knowing he needed to tell the truth, Warsaw murmured, "Um, I-I'm not sure." He felt Urskin thread his fingers into his short hair and use the hold to urge him to lift it. Giving in, Warsaw tipped his head up. He saw Urskin's questioning look and admitted, "That blew my mind, and we didn't even do anything." Then he had to share, "But I'm still hard as nails." Grimacing, Warsaw asked, "Is that normal?"

Considering he'd never had much of a sex drive for women, and he'd never allowed himself to give in to his arousal for a man, he just didn't know.

"Even with me being your mate, I would have thought

you'd have a few minutes of relief," Urskin told him, his brows furrowing, expressing his concern just as his scent did. A second later, his brows shot up. "Oh, except . . . the paste."

"The paste?" Warsaw forced himself to ask even as he began rocking his hips. His cock throbbed with a renewed need for friction, and he couldn't seem to help himself. Warsaw panted softly as he asked, "What's that mean?"

As Warsaw moved, he felt Urskin spread his legs wider. He also rocked his hips. The position change added to the pressure, and Warsaw groaned roughly.

Tingles spread through his cock's length, and a shudder racked his body.

"Damn, you're wound tight," Urskin muttered, gripping his upper arms as he rutted against him. "Should have stopped you from tasting the paste."

"Wh-Why?"

Warsaw wasn't totally sure he cared as he chased his next orgasm. He could practically feel his tingling balls begin to tighten. His lover dug his fingers into his arms as he pushed up against him, giving him that little extra bit of pressure that he needed.

With a groan, Warsaw saw stars. His release surged through him once again, and his erection pulsed more seed between their bodies. Shuddering and trembling in Urskin's hold, he panted harshly as he flew on the endorphins of his release.

Gasping, Warsaw tried to catch his breath. He blinked quickly, working to clear the spots dancing across his vision. Lifting his hand, Warsaw did his best to ignore the tremble as he rested it on Urskin's shoulder so he could do a little petting of his own.

"Gods," Warsaw muttered. "I-I . . ." He would have felt embarrassed, but his body still felt on fire. His head continued to spin with need, and his mouth watered with his desire to sink his canines back into Urskin's shoulder. Confused, Warsaw would forever deny the whine in his voice. "U-Urskin."

"Take whatever you need, my familiar," Urskin purred into his ear, rubbing down his spine. "The paste contained my blood and a powdered herb designed for the consumer to produce extra blood. In this case, it was so Jasmine could replenish her body once I healed her injuries." With a nip to his ear, Urskin continued to explain, "You ate several dollops of it, so you're producing more blood than you usually would." To Warsaw's surprise, Urskin chuckled, the sound husky, low, and going straight to Warsaw's balls. "Where do you think all that extra blood is settling?"

The answer hit Warsaw, and he groaned. "Fuck! My dick."

"Exactly." Urskin moved a hand to the back of Warsaw's neck. "It was my oversight, and I'm sorry you're paying for it." With a scoff, Urskin added, "It sounds uncomfortable, so please, do whatever you need to do to ease your ache."

Warsaw had already begun rocking his hips again by the time Urskin finished his explanation. A fresh wave of tingles began to warm him from the inside out. He felt sweat break out on his skin as he flushed hot.

Unfortunately, the cum from his first couple of releases was beginning to dry and rubbed uncomfortably on the skin of his erection. Wincing, he slowed his movements. He grimaced and forced his body to still. A tremble worked through him, and he struggled with what to do.

"Relax, Warsaw," Urskin urged with a squeeze to his neck. "Roll onto your back. Let me help you."

Warsaw blew out a breath. Jerking a nod, he focused on Urskin, waiting. When his mate pressed at his shoulders, Warsaw recalled his words and rolled to his back.

Immediately, the streaks of white coating Urskin's dark flesh drew Warsaw's attention. His breath caught in his throat as a rush of pride flooded him. He'd put that there . . . marked his mate with his seed, causing Urskin to carry his scent.

"Mmmm, you do like that you've marked me," Urskin commented, his tone holding amusement.

Snapping his attention to Urskin's face, Warsaw saw the pleasure twinkling in the man's black eyes. He couldn't help his own answering smile. His lover—*gods, I have a male lover . . . and a mate*—winked before easing down his body, alternating between skimming his palms and scraping his fingernails over his torso as he went.

"Definitely happy to help you with this," Urskin crooned as he wrapped his long fingers around the base of his erection, drawing a hiss from Warsaw. "Let's see about easing you a little more, my shifter."

Then the warlock lowered his head, opened his mouth, and wrapped his lips around Warsaw's erection, swallowing him damn near to the root.

Warsaw barked a cry as the best kind of tension caused his body to arch. Feeling Urskin pull partway off, sucking strongly, he groaned the man's name. The best kind of pleasure curdled in his gut.

"Ursk!"

Twisting his fingers in the comforter, Warsaw shuddered under his lover's ministrations. He would have felt jealous of the man's obvious skill. Except, Warsaw knew that he would be the recipient of his abilities from that day forward.

Even as Warsaw wondered if he would ever become half as good at pleasuring Urskin, he felt his balls begin to draw up once more. Butterflies bumped within his belly. His heart pounded in his chest. Even spots danced across his vision as wet suction tormented his erection in the best way possible.

Being a large man, even the few times that Warsaw had decided to hook-up with a woman, oftentimes, as soon as she'd seen the size of Warsaw's cock, she would offer to jack him off instead. His thick length was definitely intimidating.

Urskin didn't seem to have any of those hang-ups. Warsaw's mate appeared to easily take him, sinking down and sucking back up again, over and over.

Warsaw breathed deeply, roughly, unable to tear his gaze away from the arresting view of Urskin blowing him. Even as he did his best to control himself, he could feel his balls begin to draw up. He gritted his teeth and gripped the comforter tighter, reveling in the exquisite sensations thrumming through his body.

Wanting the sensations to last as long as possible, Warsaw tried to think of something other than the delicious feeling heating his groin. Except, he couldn't look at anything other than the gorgeous black man offering him the greatest fellatio of his life. Then the movement of Urskin's arm caught Warsaw's attention.

"A-Are you prepping yourself?"

Warsaw would forever deny the husky squeak that managed to creep into his voice. With the way the man's left arm was positioned behind him, he knew he couldn't be doing anything else. While Warsaw had never had sex with a man, he knew the basic principle . . . sort of.

When Urskin managed to smirk around his mouthful of Warsaw's cock, coupled with his wink, Warsaw knew it was a losing battle. With a groan, he came . . . again.

Arching, Warsaw thrust his hips up on instinct. To his surprise—and relief—Urskin didn't complain. His mate continued to suck him, even teasing his fingertips over his balls, and he groaned once more, and the spots dancing across his vision fuzzed his brain to black.

Warsaw roused, confusion filling him for an instant. Inhaling deeply, he blinked a few times. He felt something soft, warm, and wet glide across his abdominals.

Tipping his chin down, Warsaw spotted Urskin kneeling

beside him. His mate was running a damp cloth over his skin, obviously cleaning him up. He took in the dark man's serene and relaxed expression, telling him that he didn't seem to mind that Warsaw had passed out on him.

His head moving must have caught Urskin's attention. The man lifted his attention and smiled at him. "Welcome back, Warsaw." He winked as a smug grin curved his full lips. "Your responses stroke my ego."

"Your ego deserves to be stroked," Warsaw commented honestly. "You have skills."

Once again, Warsaw felt that niggle of the little green monster.

Somehow, Urskin must have picked up on it. He tossed the cloth aside before crawling forward. Pausing, half hovering over him without actually touching him, Urskin pinned him with a narrow-eyed gaze.

"Those skills are all yours for the rest of our days."

Instantly, Warsaw's unexpected ire eased. He let out a relieved breath. "Thanks." Then he sobered. "Unfortunately, I can't offer you many skills like that in return."

"If you wish to learn, I'll teach you."

Warsaw nodded. "I'd like that," he admitted honestly.

Seeing Urskin's smile, Warsaw realized he wanted a taste of that. He'd never been into kissing before, but those had all been with women. Warsaw wanted—hell, he hoped—it would be different with his mate.

Reaching up, Warsaw cradled Urskin's jaw with his right hand. He teased his thumb along the edge of the man's goatee, getting a feel for facial hair under his palm. With his other hand, Warsaw gripped Urskin's upper arm.

For several seconds, Warsaw just stared into Urskin's dark eyes, seeing the patience within their black depths.

"Come here," Warsaw finally whispered, using his hold to urge him closer. "Want to kiss you."

Urskin didn't question him. Instead, he gave in to Warsaw's tugs. As soon as Urskin's mouth pressed against Warsaw's, he nipped at those full lips.

When Urskin opened to him, Warsaw plunged his tongue inside. The man's masculine flavor burst across his taste buds. Pleasurable heat erupted through him, spreading from his mouth throughout the rest of his body.

With a groan, Warsaw pulled Urskin to him, tugging him flush against him. As he plundered his lover's mouth, learning and mapping him, he felt his body roar to life once more.

Oh, by the gods, he's perfect!

This is what passion is supposed to feel like.

CHAPTER SIX

While surprised at Warsaw's desire, Urskin went with the kiss. Some considered kissing even more intimate than sex, and he hadn't thought the big man would be ready for that for some time to come. Urskin certainly hadn't thought he would dive into it so eagerly.

But he was damn pleased to be wrong.

Relishing the needy grunts and moans escaping Warsaw — sounds Urskin was certain his familiar wasn't even aware he was making — he hung on for the ride. He accepted his shifter's eager tongue and relaxed into the man's ravishing. Feeling the man's hands rove over his upper arms, shoulders, and back, Urskin arched into the firm caresses, enjoying his man's rough explorations.

Urskin rested some of his weight on his left forearm, finding himself half-sprawled over the larger man's torso and side. His half-hard cock pressed into Warsaw's hip, springing to full mast in seconds. Unable to help himself, Urskin rocked his hips, sliding his throbbing shaft over Warsaw's smooth flesh.

When Warsaw tugged him, urging him to sprawl over his wide body more fully, Urskin found himself straddling the other man's thick waist. He felt an answering erection press along the crease of his ass. Having seen the massive tool Warsaw sported, Urskin instinctively clenched his chute muscles.

As Urskin eased the kiss to an end, his lungs screaming for relief, he focused on relaxing his body. When their lips parted, he rubbed his goateed jaw against Warsaw's smooth cheek.

Sliding his palms down the shifter's upper arms, Urskin drew in one harsh breath after another, enjoying his familiar's masculine aroma as he caught his breath.

"Urskin," Warsaw whispered, his voice just as harsh as he, too, struggled to catch his breath. "I—"

Feeling his shifter's fingers dig into his shoulder blade and one ass cheek, Urskin lifted his head. He met Warsaw's pale blue eyes, eyes glazed with need, desire, and lust. His familiar's cheeks were flushed, and his lips were kiss-swollen.

Gorgeous, handsome man.

Seeing the crease in Warsaw's brows, Urskin kept that thought to himself. He felt his lover's rod slide against his crease once more. When Warsaw opened his mouth, then closed it again, only to rut again, Urskin understood his struggle.

"How do you want me?" As soon as the words were out of Urskin's throat, he realized they were the wrong ones. Warsaw stared up at him with confusion blooming across his reddening features, and Urskin quickly amended, "Do you want hands and knees? I can lean back and ride you just like this. Or we can roll over so you're on top?"

Warsaw hesitated, his mouth opening and closing. His nostrils flared, and Urskin could imagine that he was running through all those scenarios in his mind. The shifter's eyes dilated, and he ran his palms over Urskin's sides.

"L-Like this," Warsaw replied, surprising Urskin once again. After licking his lower lip, he rumbled, "I-I'm a big guy. And I don't want to hurt you." Warsaw hesitated a heartbeat before adding, "You're beautiful. Want to see all of you riding my cock."

Urskin smiled warmly at Warsaw, pleasure filling him. "We can do that," he whispered, beyond pleased to hear not only the compliment but the shifter's concern.

After all, Warsaw was damn big.

Warsaw's smile held a mixture of anticipation and relief.

Remembering that Warsaw had zero experience with a male, Urskin reached over and grabbed the lube. He'd left it on the comforter after his familiar had passed out from pleasure. Cleaning up his shifter had been a special kind of treat, allowing him to admire and touch without the burning need overtaking Warsaw's senses.

Awake once more, Warsaw's need had returned.

And I plan to sate it, whatever it takes.

Urskin moved to rise to a kneeling position, but Warsaw's hold on him stopped him. Meeting his shifter's gaze, seeing the worry filling his expressive blue eyes, he assured, "I'm going to adjust our positions a little and grease up your erection."

Warsaw swallowed so hard his Adam's apple bobbed. His lips parted in a harsh breath. He jerked a single nod before releasing his grip on Urskin's back and ass.

Rising to his knees, Urskin popped the cap and poured a liberal amount of slick onto his palm. After closing it, he set it aside. He peered down at Warsaw's thick erection, seeing the bead of pre-cum oozing from the slit, betraying his familiar's need. His mouth watered at the sight, recalling what his handsome shifter tasted like.

Urskin gripped Warsaw's rod, his long fingers just managing to make it all the way around his shifter's hefty girth. His chute muscles twitched again, but he reminded himself that they were made for each other. Urskin knew his lover would fit.

It'll just take a little patience.

I hope he'll give that to me.

Jacking Warsaw's erection slowly, Urskin reveled in the groan of pleasure the move drew from the big blond's throat. His back arched, and he jerked into Urskin's touch. Urskin sped up his ministrations, coating his lover swiftly, seeing the feral light beginning to fill his eyes.

"You're killing me," Warsaw whined, his hips jerking beneath him. "Urskin, please."

"Try to relax, Warsaw," Urskin crooned, placing his other hand on his familiar's abdominals. He petted him soothingly as he released his lover's slicked-up prick. "Almost ready."

Warsaw nodded, his eyes taking on a glazed expression as he watched Urskin reach behind himself. As his lover's lips parted on his panting breaths, Urskin eased one finger inside his chute, then two, then a third. He'd been loosening himself earlier, prior to Warsaw passing out, and he only needed a moment until he could ease a fourth finger into his channel.

After a few passes, Urskin felt sweat pop out on his forehead. His gut clenched, and his erection twitched, tapping eagerly against his stomach. Knowing he was as ready as he was going to get, Urskin eased his fingers free.

Then Urskin shuffled forward a little, getting into the position he wanted. He gripped the base of Warsaw's erection and guided it to his hole. As Urskin touched the man's crown to his entrance, he noticed the shudder that rippled through Warsaw's body and knew his shifter was barely holding it together.

"Relax and breathe," Urskin encouraged, continuing to pet his familiar's delineated abdominals. They were truly a thing of beauty. "Focus on that as I bear down on you."

Urskin waited a few seconds, and finally, Warsaw snapped his gaze to his face. His shifter must have realized that he'd been waiting for a response, for he jerked another nod. He even managed to gasp a one-word agreement.

After Urskin saw Warsaw take a deep breath, he used his body weight to press down on his shifter's wide, flared head. He focused on relaxing and pushing out. After one heartbeat, then two, his muscles relaxed and opened, and Warsaw's large crown popped into his body.

Unable to help himself, Urskin froze. He tensed for just an

instant before he could control himself. Even seeing and touching the man's thick girth hadn't completely prepared him for the burn of the stretch.

Hearing Warsaw's whine, Urskin dragged in a deep breath of his own. He forced his body to relax as he peered down at the man Fate had deemed his. The look of pain mixed with wonder on the big man's features was a sight to behold.

Warsaw stared at where they were joined, his attention riveted to his groin. His eyes were dilated wide, and his lips were parted just a smidge. With each breath Warsaw took, denoted by the movement of his wide chest, his nostrils flared. There was even a little pain in Warsaw's eyes, but instead of moving, he twisted his thick fingers into the comforter beneath him.

Knowing what Warsaw needed, Urskin had every intention of giving it to him. After all, it was exactly what he needed, too. Urskin felt his magick sizzling beneath the surface of his skin, telling him exactly how close he was to losing control for the first time in . . . longer than he could recall.

After one more deep breath, Urskin let it out slowly between pursed lips. At the same time, he used his body weight to sink down, down, onto Warsaw's greased pole. Finally, after what felt like an extremely long time, Urskin felt Warsaw's groin hair beneath his ass cheeks and the heat of his flesh against his own.

A shudder went through Urskin. There was no doubt about it. Warsaw was huge—definitely the largest Urskin could ever recall taking. His gut clenched and released as he focused on staying relaxed.

With a whine, Warsaw clamped his hands onto Urskin's hips.

Urskin snapped open eyelids he hadn't even realized he'd closed. He focused on his familiar's face. Taking in the pleasure-pain that was twisting Warsaw's features, Urskin moaned in appreciation.

Tensing his thighs, Urskin prepared to lift his body, planning to draw halfway off the man's cock. To his surprise, he felt Warsaw's hands clamp tighter on him. Urskin paused, lifting his brows in silent question as he met Warsaw's gaze.

Warsaw peered up at him. "No," he muttered, shaking his head once. His brows were furrowed, and he swallowed hard. "D-Don't move."

Resting his hands over Warsaw's, Urskin massaged the man's tense fingers gently. "Why, my familiar?" he crooned. "What's wrong?"

His features twisting, Warsaw admitted, "Feels so good. Too good." A whining strain filled his voice. "Never felt anything like it." His tongue flicked out, and a shudder worked through the big body beneath Urskin. "G-Gonna come."

"Then come, Warsaw," Urskin encouraged, tightening and loosening his chute muscles as he spoke. He grinned when Warsaw sucked in a sharp breath, and he told him, "It's what you need, my familiar. You *need* to come." Leaning forward, Urskin moved his palms up to Warsaw's nipples. He held Warsaw's gaze as he gave the small nubs an experimental squeeze. At the same time, Urskin clenched around his lover's invading member once more as he tipped his head to the side and hissed, "Take your pleasure, Warsaw. Mark your mate."

Warsaw groaned before doing exactly as Urskin bid. As his lover slid his hands up his body, he crunched up. Wrapping his arms around Urskin's torso, Warsaw gripped his shoulder blades and yanked him forward.

A second later, Urskin felt Warsaw's teeth pierce the mark he'd left where his neck met his shoulder. He hissed, then moaned as, just as he remembered, the sweetest tingles of bliss erupted. They spread across his skin, moving down his torso. Urskin's nipples beaded, and his stomach muscles fluttered.

Urskin moaned Warsaw's name as his orgasm rushed through his body. His cock erupted, sending hard shudders through him in ecstasy-inducing spurts. He felt Warsaw rock his hips, sinking just a smidge deeper into Urskin's body.

A second later, even through Urskin's bliss, he registered the hard shudder that went through the body below him. He felt the stretch in his channel as Warsaw's erection swelled. The hot seed soaking his inner walls pulled a moan from him, experiencing a first with his familiar. Urskin groaned again as another burst of hot goodness coated his inner walls, heating him from the inside out in a way that he knew would always feel unique.

"Warsaw," Urskin muttered, pleasure infusing him. His magick swelled within his veins, and beams of light ricocheted off the walls, only to return and wrap them both in a shimmering cocoon. "My familiar."

Warsaw gasped, the move pulling the shifter's teeth from his neck. "Urskin," he whispered gruffly, freezing beneath him.

"Relax, my familiar," Urskin crooned, rubbing up and down Warsaw's side. "This is normal." Feeling the pleasant tingles of his magick reaching out to Warsaw, as well as to the man's animal, Urskin closed his eyes and hummed. He could see the lines of their bond strengthening between them. The glow of his power wrapped around Warsaw's soul, and in Urskin's mind, he could practically see the shifter's buffalo prance within the light. "Gods, your soul is gorgeous."

For a long moment, Warsaw lay quiet beneath him. His hands had stilled on Urskin's back, although his fingers did twitch. His chest rose and fell beneath him, and the shifter's warm breath ghosted across his neck.

When the silence stretched out for one moment, then two, Urskin finally eased his head to the side enough to peer at Warsaw. He saw the shifter's furrowed brows and the clench to his jaw. Even his blue eyes appeared a little vacant.

A second later, Urskin felt his magick settle back within him, the glow in the room returning to normal.

"Warsaw?" Urskin glided his hands up Warsaw's arms to rest on his neck. He caressed over the shifter's prominent Adam's apple. "You with me?"

After a grunt, Warsaw blinked and turned his attention to Urskin's face. "Yeah." Squinting at him, he murmured, "You can see my soul?"

Urskin sobered. "Not in the sense you mean," he replied, taking a chance and pressing a light kiss to Warsaw's lips. "I see your aura, but I've always found a person's aura to be a pretty good representative of a person's soul, and your aura is a beautiful color." Then Urskin grimaced and admitted, "Although, I do see the lines of sadness through it." Urskin barely resisted asking about the reason behind that, figuring Warsaw would explain when he was ready.

Warsaw grunted before tucking his face against Urskin's neck. Without a word, he landed a hand on Urskin's ass as he began rocking his hips. Warsaw lapped over Urskin's flesh as he slowly rutted into him, closing the claiming wound he'd left open a moment prior.

To Urskin's pleasure, Warsaw began sliding over his prostate, and his brain began to shut down as arousal surged through him once more.

Welcoming Warsaw's attention, Urskin relaxed into his ministrations, relishing the sound of soft masculine grunts, the smell of musky need, and the feel of a sweaty male body beneath him.

CHAPTER SEVEN

"I've never held anyone after sex."

The words were out of Warsaw's mouth before he could think better of them. Wincing, he peered pensively down at the man he spooned in his arms. After their first couple of rounds, they'd shifted into another position. One where Warsaw and Urskin lay on their sides, with Warsaw's chest to Urskin's back.

Warsaw had loved cradling the smaller man, even as he'd petted Urskin's strong, firm muscles. The way the man let him slowly saw his dick in and out of his body in long, languorous strokes had been the icing on the cake. Even after Warsaw had come, biting Urskin's neck and taking him with him, he hadn't pulled out, and Urskin hadn't asked him to.

Instead, Warsaw held Urskin close, still embedded within him. Although his erection had softened to half-mast.

Finally.

To Warsaw's relief, Urskin let out a soft, rumbling chuckle. He turned his head just enough to peer at Warsaw over his shoulder. "Considering your cock is still in me, is this truly considered *after sex*?"

Warsaw smiled back at the man and shrugged one shoulder. "Dunno."

Resting his head on the pillow he shared with Urskin, he nuzzled the older man's nape as he inhaled deeply. Warsaw couldn't seem to get enough of his mate's scent. There was a wild masculine quality to it that sent his senses soaring. Warsaw agreed with his buffalo, and he just wanted to wallow in it.

"Well, this is the part where we talk a little and share a bit about ourselves with each other," Urskin told him, his tenor voice sounding soft and relaxed. "Past relationships. Problems with parents, siblings, or kids if we have them. That sort of thing."

After so many orgasms, Warsaw felt sated and sleepy. "Really?" He'd never been in a relationship, so he would have to defer to Urskin's knowledge. "Well, I'm one hundred-forty-two, and my parents died when I was a child. I was raised by Kennedy's parents, but they're dead now, too." Sighing deeply, Warsaw muttered, "So's Kennedy."

"Kennedy," Urskin repeated slowly. "He was like a brother to you."

Warsaw rested his forehead against Urskin's nape, clutching him close. "Yeah," he conceded. Squeezing Urskin's torso lightly, he admitted, "He wouldn't have agreed with this. He was a homophobe."

"I'm sorry to hear that," Urskin replied softly. "That's why you were in the closet?"

"Yeah. Partly."

"Partly? Until when?" Urskin peered at Warsaw over his shoulder, his black brows furrowed just a little. "Because you're obviously not now." After a second of hesitation, Urskin asked astutely, "Is it because Kennedy is deceased?"

Sighing sadly, Warsaw shook his head. "Naw. Was in the closet because I loved someone I couldn't have. He'd already found his fated mate." Scoffing, Warsaw muttered, "Didn't see the point of ruining my friendship with Kennedy when I could never have the guy I wanted. Ya know?"

Warsaw wondered if it was bad form to tell his own fated mate about someone else he was in love with, but Urskin had said they were supposed to share their past. Besides, his mate needed to know why he wasn't about to fall in love with him in seconds like Warsaw had seen so many other shifters do with their mates.

Urskin hummed softly for a few seconds, perhaps processing his words. "And where is this man now?"

"He's dead, too. Him and his mate," Warsaw whispered, grimacing. "His mate died in the battle with the rogues, so he followed her shortly after."

"Ah. That's normally the way of fated mates," Urskin murmured, sounding commiserating. "They say it's so the Fates can reincarnate their spirits in close proximity, so they can find each other in the next life."

"You said normally." Warsaw wondered about that. "Why normally? Doesn't it always happen?"

Urskin lifted a hand from the bed before him and waggled it back and forth. "I've heard of a few cases where the relationship of the fated pair was not good, so the second person lived on after their partner passed." After a second of silence, Urskin added, "There were children involved, so the remaining parent had something else to live for."

"Oh." Warsaw figured that made sense. Except—"Why was their relationship strained? Was the human not a good person and took advantage of their partner's paranormal nature?"

"Actually, the other way around," Urskin told him, surprising Warsaw. "The paranormal ended up in bad company. He listened to very poor advice, went against his nature, and treated his mate badly."

"Damn." Warsaw frowned and even shook his head in surprise and a little disbelief, but he could scent Urskin's truthfulness. "I may not love you, but I'll never purposefully treat you badly," Warsaw declared, nuzzling Urskin's neck.

Urskin chuckled softly as he tilted his head, giving Warsaw more room. "Good to know, my familiar. Good to know."

After licking Urskin's skin, enjoying the slightly salty flavor, Warsaw stated, "You mentioned loving someone once. What happened to him?" Realizing he was making an assumption, Warsaw quickly amended, "Or her?"

Turning his head, Urskin met his gaze. "I've loved both, Warsaw," he told him frankly. "At over three hundred years, I've been in several relationships." Continuing to eye him, Urskin stated, "I'm going to roll over now, Warsaw. I'd like to have this conversation face-to-face. Is that okay with you?"

Warsaw nodded, realizing talking about relationships was probably a serious topic. When Urskin eased from his hold, he immediately felt the loss, and it wasn't because his dick slipped from his mate's warm body. Instead, Warsaw found that his arms felt empty as he watched Urskin roll to face him.

I want to hold him again.

Deciding to act on his need — after all, Urskin would tell him if he didn't like it — Warsaw slid his arm under the smaller male. He rolled to his back while tugging his human with him. Once Warsaw had Urskin sprawled half over him, he grabbed the comforter from where it had been shoved to the side of the bed at some point. After tugging it over them both, Warsaw sighed and relaxed once more.

Rubbing his palms up and down Urskin's warm back, Warsaw stated, "I'm not sure why, but I like holding you." He peered into Urskin's black eyes. "I hope you don't mind."

Urskin chuckled softly, his dark lips curving enticingly. "I enjoy being held," he told him. Then he smirked. "Of course, being the smaller of a pair will take some getting used to, but I'm certainly not complaining."

Warsaw nodded.

Good.

"My magick began surfacing when I hit puberty, which is normal for a warlock," Urskin explained. "A man named Morgan came into my life. He bought me from my owner, and he became my mentor. I was born a slave, you see. I tutored under Morgan for nearly three decades." With a wince, Urskin told him, "I used the Civil War as a way to die to everyone who knew me, and I started my life as a nomad. For the first few decades, Morgan traveled with me, but he soon went his own way."

"Do you still speak to him?" Warsaw asked curiously. His mind boggled a little. "Did you really partake in the Civil War?"

"No, Morgan is deceased. Three hundred years is getting up there for a warlock," Urskin explained. "And I did not fight in the Civil War," Urskin answered with a grimace. His black brows furrowed as he admitted, "I would have been far too tempted to use magick to help the Union win, and Morgan had warned me over and over about the dangers of allowing my personal feelings to change the course of fate."

Warsaw nodded slowly. "Okay. I guess I can see that." He realized his mate had to have had one hell of a moral compass because he wasn't certain he would have had that much self-control. "So you traveled instead." Taking a guess, Warsaw added, "Away from the fighting, I'd wager."

"Yes," Urskin confirmed. "I went west, searching for my familiar. Morgan had told me stories about not only the connection I'd feel to a familiar but the boost it would give to my abilities." His smile turned wry as he peered up at Warsaw. "Of course, I never found you, seeing as you hadn't been born yet."

Chuckling, Warsaw nodded as he felt his cheeks heat a little. "Sorry."

Urskin shrugged one lean shoulder. "I found my diversions, and yes, that included love a couple of times. The first was with a widowed ranch woman. Lydia. Of course, interracial couples were frowned upon, even out west, so whenever anyone asked, I was always introduced as her hired hand." With a scoff, Urskin continued, "That was true of the man I fell for a few years before the first World War, too. Laramie. He introduced me as his friend even though we were so much more behind closed doors."

"Damn. That had to suck." Warsaw growled under his breath, doing his best to squash his rising surge of jealousy. "Damn prejudices."

"They were different times back then," Urskin commented softly, his expression turning sad. "They weren't my familiar, but I still mourned their passings."

"How'd they die?" The words were out of Warsaw's mouth before he could stop himself. Wincing, he quickly added, "You don't have to tell me."

"Lydia died when she came off a horse, or so I was told," Urskin replied, his voice growing soft as his expression turned reflective. "I was out rounding up a few stray cattle. Otherwise, I probably would have been able to save her."

"I'm sorry," Warsaw repeated.

Urskin shrugged his slender shoulder again. "It was a long time ago."

"That doesn't mean you don't miss them," Warsaw pointed out.

"Time does dull the ache, though," Urskin told him, rubbing Warsaw's chest. "Anyway, Laramie didn't know I was a warlock. His faith in The Almighty meant he thought anything even resembling witchcraft was of the devil, so I kept that from him. When he was drafted for the war, he didn't understand why I wouldn't offer to sign up, too." Scoffing, Urskin revealed, "Little did Laramie know that I wasn't actually in the system anywhere, seeing as I was born over two centuries before."

"What happened?" Warsaw couldn't help but ask.

Urskin sighed, his brows furrowing as a gleam of sadness filled his dark eyes. "We separated, and he died overseas. His body was returned to his mother."

"Damn." Warsaw's heart ached for Urskin. "I'm sorry."

Humming softly, Urskin repeated, "It was a long time ago."

Warsaw pressed his lips together, knowing a platitude was pointless. Instead, he petted up and down Urskin's back, hoping to ease the tension he felt in the older man. In all his dreams of having a mate—and after falling for Damian, that hadn't been too often—it had never occurred to him that his mate would be older, with a shit-ton more experience.

He wasn't entirely certain what to say.

Urskin pinched his nipple.

Hissing, Warsaw frowned at Urskin. "Ow," he grumbled.

Smirking, Urskin stated, "I didn't tell you all that to bring down the mood."

"Then why?" Warsaw widened his eyes as a thought struck. "Oh, because you said this is when people starting a relationship share their pasts."

"Partly," Urskin confirmed. "But it was also to explain that I understand the pain of losing someone you love, even if you're not in a relationship with that person at the time." He smiled as he rubbed his thumb over Warsaw's abused nipple, soothing the sting he'd caused. "When I learned of Laramie's death, even though we were no longer in a relationship, I still mourned him. Just as you are not in a position to offer me love because you're mourning Damian, I wouldn't have been in a position to offer immediate love if I'd met my familiar at that time." Urskin rubbed a warm palm over Warsaw's torso soothingly. "So, we offer each other friendship, companionship, and we build our lives from there."

Warsaw nodded. "Thank you."

Before Warsaw could think of anything else to say, his stomach grumbled . . . loudly.

Urskin chuckled. "Guess it's time to eat."

"Are you hungry?" Warsaw asked, refusing to loosen his

grip when Urskin shifted as if to pull away from him. "I can wait."

Warsaw was enjoying holding Urskin. He'd never experienced the simple intimacy of cuddling in afterglow.

"I wouldn't mind a meal," Urskin told him, even as he settled against Warsaw once more. "But we can wait until you're ready."

Hesitating, Warsaw tried to decide what to do—stay hungry and hold his mate or get food to feed them both. Then Urskin's stomach growled, too. His instinct to see to his mate's needs kicked in hard.

"We should get up," Warsaw stated, unable to hide his disappointment. "I normally eat after my shift on the grounds crew, and well"—he felt his cheeks heat—"that didn't happen this time around because, uhhhh."

"Because you met your mate," Urskin finished for him, a relaxed smile curving his dark lips as he eased into a sitting position. His black eyes glimmered in the bedroom light as he swept his gaze over Warsaw's nude form. "And you became distracted in the most enjoyable of ways."

Warsaw felt a mixture of embarrassment and pride upon seeing Urskin's open appreciation. "Yeah," he grunted as he slid off the bed. Turning back to Urskin, he held out his hand, offering to help his mate from his bed. As the warlock accepted his assistance, Warsaw returned the man's open perusal. "And I figure I'm gonna get distracted plenty in the future, too."

The smile that creased Urskin's lips called to Warsaw, and he couldn't resist. He dipped his head and pressed his mouth to the warlock's. When Urskin immediately opened to him, Warsaw groaned roughly and began to deepen the kiss.

Then both their stomachs rumbled.

While Warsaw groaned, Urskin chuckled. The handsome

black man eased from his hold and headed toward the bathroom. "I'd invite you to join me, but then we'd probably never eat," his mate stated before closing the door with a wink.

Figuring his mate was right, Warsaw headed to the kitchenette to clean up.

Fifteen minutes later, Warsaw felt a fissure of nerves tingle up his spine as he led the way into the dining hall. He hadn't had much in his refrigerator, so he'd opted to take his hungry mate to the massive room where food was offered free of charge to all shifters and other employees. At the time, Warsaw hadn't thought much about it.

Except, when Warsaw opened the door for Urskin, he spotted Enforcer Richmond sitting with Lonnie. Gretchen, Richmond's gazelle shifter mate by choice, sat beside him. Next to Lonnie sat the tiger shifter he was currently dating, Rita.

All four pinned Warsaw with varying looks of disgust.

Great.

Warsaw did his best to ignore the group as he led the way toward the buffet. "If you don't find what you'd like up here, you can place a specialty order at that window," Warsaw told Urskin, pointing.

"I'm not a picky man," Urskin replied. "I'm sure—"

"Hey, asshole," Lonnie snarled, rising from his chair.

Richmond did the same, obviously backing him.

Focusing on reaching the buffet, Warsaw did his best to ignore Lonnie's call. Although, he did see the pair moving toward him, so he figured that wouldn't work.

"Did you just call my familiar an asshole?" Urskin stopped in the aisle and turned to face Lonnie. His black eyes held a wealth of frigid anger, appearing fathomless in the bright overhead lights. "Keep your tongue to yourself, little kitty."

CHAPTER EIGHT

Anger surged through Urskin when he realized that the blond-haired lion shifter had been directing his name-calling at Warsaw.

"Just ignore him," Warsaw urged softly, touching the small of his back. "Lonnie calls me that all the time." Lowering his voice, Warsaw whispered into his ear, "It's not worth the headache of engaging."

"That's Lonnie?"

Urskin asked for clarification, not taking his attention away from the advancing red-faced blond. In his peripheral vision, Urskin saw Warsaw nod. Upon him learning that, his anger increased. Urskin recalled Delanrue sharing how Lonnie had already accosted his familiar once that afternoon.

"What the fuck did you say to me?" Lonnie asked belligerently, stepping into Urskin's space, trying to use his inch-taller body to intimidate Urskin. "How dare you talk to me like that, fucker."

Urskin wasn't impressed. A number of spells crossed his mind, spells that would instantly put the young upstart shifter in his place. Urskin clenched his jaw, barely keeping himself from uttering one of them.

Lonnie's lip curled as he reached out a hand and pushed Urskin's shoulder, causing him to rock back a step. "Get out of here, human, if ya know what's good for ya." His expression told Urskin exactly what he thought of humans — that they were beneath him — even if the moron was mistaken about what Urskin truly was.

"Don't touch him," Warsaw growled, wrapping his arm around Urskin's waist and attempting to ease in front of him. Although Urskin did his best not to allow it. "Your beef is with me, Lonnie. Leave Urskin out of it."

Lonnie glared at Warsaw. "Then tell *Urskin* to butt out, asshole," he ordered, glancing at where Warsaw had his arm around his waist back to Warsaw's face. His nostrils flared suddenly, and he must have noticed their shared scents. Snorting, he eyed them snidely. "Can't find a shifter to let ya fuck 'em, so you're goin' for a humie." Lonnie shook his head, his expression taking on a look of cruel superiority. "Figures." A second later, his blue eyes narrowed into cold slits. "Does Urskin know you're a disgraced rogue, asshole?"

Urskin noticed the beginnings of red creeping up Warsaw's neck, but he didn't know if it was from embarrassment or anger. Either way, it pissed him off. Resting his palm on the small of his familiar's back, he eased a step forward so he was on equal footing with Warsaw.

"I told you not to call my familiar that, Lonnie," Urskin growled. His magick sizzled underneath his skin, responding to his anger. Urskin clenched his free hand to keep it in check. "Continue verbally abusing Warsaw, and I'll demand restitution."

Sneering, Lonnie declared, "You can't demand shit." He crossed his arms over his chest. "This rogue should be put down for his crimes, not be given a slap on the wrist." Then he focused on Warsaw, "And I'm gonna demand restitution from you, asshole, because you sent Delanrue after me when your mutt was attacked." Lonnie's eyes took on a crazed gleam. "Did the rat die?"

"Wait a minute." The other, larger shifter rested his hand on Lonnie's shoulder. "That's why Enforcer Delanrue hauled you in to talk?" His dark brows furrowed as he focused on

Warsaw, his expression troubled. "Someone attacked Jasmine?"

A tick formed in Warsaw's jaw as he growled, "Yeah." After a sharp inhale, he continued, "Someone attacked Jasmine, Enforcer Richmond."

"Shit," the second lion shifter — Richmond — grumbled. "Sorry to hear that. Is she okay?"

Warsaw blinked, seemingly surprised by Richmond's apparent empathy. "She's fine." His arm around Urskin tightened just a little. "Thanks to Urskin."

"Good." Richmond nodded. "That's—"

"Good?" Lonnie snapped, glaring at Richmond. "What do you mean, *good*? This is that asshole's dog" — he punctuated his words by stabbing a finger in Warsaw's direction — "we're talkin' about here."

"Jasmine's a dog." Richmond frowned at Lonnie. "It's not her fault her owner's a dick."

Aaaand there goes all the goodwill I was starting to have for this guy.

"That's enough," Urskin snarled. Pointing a finger between the pair, he warned, "Call Warsaw one more name, and I'll—"

"You'll what?" Lonnie cut in with a snort. "Whatcha gonna do, humie? Whatcha gonna do when I call your fuck-buddy an asshole?"

"This."

Urskin spread his fingers and bent his wrist so his palm was facing Lonnie. As he muttered a few words, he pumped his hand toward the annoying shifter's chest.

Without a touch, Lonnie went flying across the dining hall. He slammed into the wall on the far side, about halfway up, with a resounding crack. Slumping to the floor, Lonnie left a body-sized dent in the drywall.

"What the hell?" Richmond roared, pivoting to face him again. His dark eyes were wide in his face for another second before they narrowed. He growled and tensed, obviously ready to attack. "You're under arrest for attacking a shifter without provocation."

Urskin knew Warsaw had been right. It really would have been better to just keep walking. Except, he'd encountered these types of jackasses from coast to coast. The only way to deal with them was with force.

But the aftermath will definitely be annoying.

"Unprovoked attack, my ass," Urskin replied drolly. He flicked his finger toward the downed Lonnie. "He pushed me and insulted me and my familiar . . . repeatedly." With a scoff, Urskin added, "Lonnie's lucky all I did was toss him across the room."

As Urskin spoke, he noticed the redhead who'd been at the table with the pair go racing across the dining hall to check on Lonnie. The blonde rushed to Richmond's side. Her blue eyes blazed with anger, and her aura was streaked with grays of hate and a vicious need for vengeance.

Damn. Not a nice woman.

"Your level of violence was uncalled for," Richmond insisted, a growl in his voice. "Come quietly. Don't make me restrain you."

Urskin scoffed. "You can't restrain me, young lion. Contact Head Enforcer Mycroft or one of the Drudeson brothers," he ordered. "I'll answer only to them."

Shaking his head, Urskin did something he should have done in the first place. He slipped his hand into his trench coat. When Urskin had donned it before leaving the room, Warsaw had cocked his head in silent question, but he'd kept his thoughts to himself.

Now Urskin appreciated the foresight.

After pulling a small vial from one of many hidden pockets, Urskin quickly uncorked it. He poured some of the powder into his hand. As Urskin did that, he urged Warsaw to the left, putting a little bit of space between them and the wary —

and angry — shifters.

Just as Richmond started advancing on them, even as he waved for the blonde to stay back, Urskin tossed the powder into the air. He quickly uttered a spell. The yellow particles glowed in the air as they fell, coating Urskin and Warsaw.

A second later, five feet from them, Richmond stopped. He appeared to bounce off of . . . something. Rubbing his shoulder with one hand, a scowl marring his features, Richmond lifted his other hand and placed it on an invisible wall.

Urskin met Richmond's angry gaze through his shield.

"What the hell?" Richmond roared. Making a fist, he slammed it on the shield wall. "Lower this right the fuck now, warlock."

"Well, that's better than being called humie." Urskin glanced Warsaw's way, smirking. "Shall we get something to eat? I'm ready for a meal."

Warsaw gaped at Urskin. His blue eyes were wide in his face, and his cheeks appeared a little pale. He opened and closed his mouth as he glanced from Urskin to Richmond and back again.

"Wh-What?"

Urskin realized he'd shocked his familiar just as much as the others in the dining hall. He still had so much to explain to his shifter. Having lived so long, Urskin had learned, crafted, and perfected many abilities.

Guess I'll need to tell him about them.

We haven't really had a chance, yet.

"Come on, Warsaw," Urskin urged, turning the bigger man away from the still-shouting and angry lion shifter. "I've erected a force field, of sorts." Urskin really didn't know what else to call it. "It'll keep them out for a while so we can enjoy a meal."

Urskin's stomach growled once more, reminding him of just how hungry he was. Using magick had only increased his need. He figured using magick was like shifting, in that way.

Doing it often was hard on the body, burning calories swiftly.

"Uh, okay."

To Urskin's pleasure, Warsaw allowed him to guide him to the table of food. He grabbed two plates as well as rolls of utensils. Then he handed one of each to his lover.

Sweeping his gaze over the buffet, Urskin took in the offerings. He chose a heaping helping of tuna pasta casserole, several pieces of fried chicken, and a large dollop of mashed potatoes and gravy. His stomach growled as the fragrance of the food teased his nostrils, and Urskin hummed in anticipation. Finally, he grabbed two large chocolate, chocolate chip cookies with a spare napkin.

"Wow." Warsaw chuckled softly. "You eat like a shifter."

Urskin smiled at Warsaw, nodding. "It's the magick in me."

Warsaw nodded, then slapped several pieces of Salisbury steak patties onto his plate, along with a couple of dollops of mashed potatoes. He topped that with plenty of gravy. Finally, Warsaw poured a layer of corn all over it.

Huh. Looks good.

"So, uh, how do we get to a table?" Warsaw asked, eyeing where Richmond stood a few feet away with his phone to his ear.

With a shrug and a wry grin, Urskin began moving to the left. "The shield extends about five feet around us, and it'll move with us." Tipping his chin toward where Richmond was already backing up a step, Urskin explained, "It'll make all living creatures move out of the way. Except for plants. They're in a different class, I guess."

Even Urskin had found there were limits to his understanding of magick.

"Okay."

After they reached a table, Urskin took a seat, placing his food before him. Warsaw sat to his left. He picked up a fried chicken leg and glanced toward the buffet.

"Huh. We forgot drinks," Urskin commented.

"What do you want?" Warsaw asked, peering toward a separate counter set up with carafes, dispensers, and several mini fridges underneath it. "I can snag something."

Urskin shook his head while resting his free hand on Warsaw's wrist. "If you leave the perimeter of the shield, you won't be able to get back in," he explained. "Unless you're desperate for a drink, leave it for now."

Warsaw nodded, picking up his knife and fork.

Urskin returned his attention to his chicken leg. As he took a big bite out of the crunchy goodness, he spotted a man bussing a table a couple away from them. From his aura, Urskin knew he was a fox shifter.

The guy discreetly peered Richmond's way, who was glancing between them and Lonnie. The arrogant lion shifter was being helped to his feet by the redhead. When Richmond focused on Lonnie once more, the fox shifter bent and rolled a couple of items toward them. As they were inanimate objects, they passed right through Urskin's shield.

For just an instant, Urskin tensed, fearing for their safety. After all, a bomb or grenade could pass through his protection. He worried he'd misread the kindness in the fox shifter's aura.

Then Urskin spotted what the fox shifter was sending them—two cans of soda. With a smile, he tipped his head in a thank-you nod. He grabbed them off the floor and placed one before Warsaw.

Warsaw looked up from his food, then the fox shifter's way. He scoffed softly as a small smile curved his lips. "That's Desmond. He works in the kitchen," he told him quietly. "Desmond's a good guy. Doesn't hold my stupidity against me."

"You were in a bad place," Urskin murmured with a squeeze to Warsaw's wrist. "We'll get through this, and life will get better."

After holding Urskin's gaze for a few heartbeats, Warsaw offered him a small smile. "Yeah. Fate sent me you." Then his cheeks took on a pinkish hue, and he returned his attention to his food.

Urskin had no desire to call attention to Warsaw's discomfort, so he followed his shifter's example. Besides, the food was amazing. Whoever made the fried chicken had an absolutely fantastic recipe. The seasonings were the perfect mixture, blending wonderfully with the soft, succulent meat.

After Urskin polished off a thigh section, he wiped his hands on his napkin. He grabbed his fork and reached toward Warsaw's plate. Wanting to taste his familiar's concoction, Urskin eased his tines through the mashed potatoes, gravy, and corn. He finished by stabbing a small bite of Salisbury steak. Popping it into his mouth, Urskin hummed appreciatively.

His mouth still full, Urskin mumbled, "Oh, that's good."

Warsaw chuckled, amusement twinkling in his blue eyes.

Gods, that's such a better look on my familiar.

Urskin hoped to put that happiness on his shifter often.

Unfortunately, just as quickly, Warsaw's expression slipped away to be replaced by trepidation.

Following Warsaw's line of sight, Urskin spotted a group of shifters heading their way. Not only had Mycroft arrived, but so had Delanrue, Dane, and Dakota. Even Councilman Regales Colearian accompanied them.

Richmond followed, his dark eyes narrowed and jaw clenched. The blonde accompanied him, a haughty expression diminishing her attractiveness. A woozy-looking Lonnie made up the rear, being helped by the redhead.

Urskin didn't particularly care for Lonnie's smug expression. Fortunately, he knew he'd been well within his rights to defend not only himself, but Warsaw, too. The guy was a total tool.

Stopping five feet away from them, Mycroft lifted a hand. He tapped a knuckle on the invisible dome encasing them. Arching one red eyebrow, he smirked at Urskin.

With a couple words and a wave of his hand, Urskin removed the barrier. He smiled at the shifters that he sort of considered friends. "Hello, gentlemen." Urskin indicated the seats around the table, which could accommodate eight people. "Please, join us. We're nearly finished."

"Why you fucking asshole," Lonnie snarled, glaring daggers at him and Warsaw both.

Urskin rolled his eyes before meeting Mycroft's gaze. "He really doesn't learn, does he?"

"Afraid not," Mycroft replied. Turning his attention to the youngest brother, he ordered, "Enforcer Dakota, please escort Lonnie out of here. Put him in holding."

"Yes, sir." Dakota immediately started toward Lonnie.

Lonnie wasn't the only one to shout, "What the fuck?"

CHAPTER NINE

Warsaw stared in shock as Mycroft rounded on Lonnie and Rita, a stern expression on his wiry features. "Security footage." Holding up his phone, he allowed them to view his screen. He used a finger to indicate the space around them. "The dining hall is monitored with a number of cameras, Lonnie. I heard and saw exactly what happened, and Urskin was well within his right to put you in your place for verbally assaulting not only himself, but Warsaw . . . repeatedly." Shaking his head, Mycroft growled, "When I spoke with Enforcer Delanrue earlier, he told me that he warned you to steer clear of Warsaw." Mycroft pointed at his phone. "This is the exact opposite of steer clear. Now get him out of my sight."

Enforcer Richmond's nostrils flared, and he clenched his hands at his sides. He glanced between Gretchen and Rita, then refocused on Mycroft. "Sir, I was not aware that Lonnie had been warned away from interacting with Warsaw," he began slowly. With narrowed eyes, he continued, "However, shouldn't the fact that the warlock used excessive force be taken into account?" When Mycroft focused on Richmond, a frown marring his brows, the lion shifter quickly added, "After all, throwing him across the room —"

"Lonnie was warned," Mycroft cut in. "Repeatedly." With a scoff, he crossed his arms over his lean torso. "Maybe getting knocked upside the head a few times is exactly what he needs."

Richmond gaped, clearly shocked by Mycroft's stance. He also seemed to be at a loss for words.

Rita didn't have that problem. "What?" she screeched, a sneer twisting her lips. "That rogue mates with some damn warlock, and now, all of a sudden, he gets preferential treatment?" Rita's voice rose higher, making Warsaw's ears threaten to ring. "How is that fair?" Pointing at Warsaw, she continued, "He was hardly even punished!"

"Warsaw's punishment was handed out by the Shifter Council, Rita," Councilman Colearian stated, his voice dark and growly. "Regardless of your own personal feelings on the matter, it has been settled to our satisfaction. Leave Warsaw alone, and move on."

Rita's face flushed to the point where it nearly matched her red hair. When she went to open her mouth, Gretchen quickly grabbed her upper arm. The gazelle shifter wrapped her other arm around the tiger shifter's waist and turned her away. As Gretchen urged Rita out of the dining hall, she whispered something in the redhead's ear that made the woman nod once, something that was far too quiet for Warsaw to catch.

Councilman Colearian turned his attention to Enforcer Richmond. "I understand that those people are your mate and your friends, and I know you all lost a good friend in the battle." His tone softened, and his expression turned sad. "Damian was a friend to many. So was Madison, and they are both missed, but this conduct is unbecoming of a council enforcer, Richmond." Colearian held Richmond's gaze for several heartbeats before saying, "This matter is finished. Do you understand?"

A muscle ticked in Richmond's jaw even as he dipped his head in a sharp nod. "Yes, Councilman. I understand."

While Colearian nodded, he evidently wasn't finished. "And as a council enforcer, it's your duty to uphold our verdicts, even those you don't personally agree with." He glanced pointedly at Warsaw. "And it's your duty to either stop others from going against us or to warn us of those who do not obey."

Richmond's face darkened as the scents of embarrassment, anger, and distaste began to emanate from him. "Yes, Councilman," he repeated softly.

"Thank you, Enforcer Richmond," Councilman Colearian replied. "You're dismissed."

After dipping his head once more, Enforcer Richmond strode away. With his back straight and his shoulders back, he moved stiffly. He took his scent of disquiet with him.

Councilman Colearian turned his attention to Warsaw. To his surprise, the aging grizzly shifter smiled at him. "Congratulations on finding your mate, Warsaw. I'm truly happy for you." His expression softened. "You're definitely due for something good in your life." Reaching out, Colearian rested his hand on Warsaw's shoulder and gave it a quick squeeze before releasing him. "I was sorry to hear about Jasmine, and we won't rest until we figure out who committed such a callous and heinous act."

"Th-Thank you, Councilman," Warsaw stuttered.

In shock, Warsaw watched the councilman pat Mycroft on the shoulder. "Thanks for bringing me into the loop on this, Mycroft. Keep me posted." After Mycroft had given his confirmation, Colearian turned to Dane. "Come on, Dane. Escort me out. Theo is waiting on me."

"Of course, Regales," Dane replied, dropping formality. As he turned to follow the councilman, he glanced between Warsaw and Urskin. "Congrats to you both, guys." Then Dane reached past Councilman Colearian and opened the door for him. As they disappeared out the door, Dane asked, "You and Theo coming for poker this weekend?"

The door closed, and Warsaw missed the councilman's answer.

With a sigh, Mycroft turned to face Urskin. "I have to go

deal with Lonnie . . . again." He rolled his eyes before smirking at them. "After that, I want to hear about this ability you have to throw a shifter across the dining hall." Mycroft held up his phone. "It's impressive."

Urskin dipped his head in a small nod of acknowledgment. "Thank you." He focused on their nearly finished meals. "After we eat, we can meet you somewhere." Gently, Urskin wrapped his long fingers around Warsaw's wrist, causing the hairs on his arm to stand on end. "After that incident, I don't want to let my familiar out of my sight for a bit."

"Understandable," Mycroft conceded.

"We'll all be in my and Miggs's quarters, having a beer," Delanrue cut in, crossing his arms over his chest as if daring Warsaw to counter him. "You can pick up Jasmine and tell me just how long these guys have been harassing you."

Warsaw hesitated. He hated tattling. Except, he knew the enforcer wasn't making a request.

"Okay, sir."

Mycroft nodded. "Okay." As he turned and began heading toward the door, he called, "Save a beer for me and Boyd."

As Delanrue gave a mock salute, Warsaw reeled a little, amazed at how a few hours could change everything. He knew Boyd was Mycroft's fairly newly bonded vampire mate, even though he'd never met the man.

And now, I'm about to have a beer with the top enforcers working for the shifter council.

When Warsaw agreed to have a beer when stopping by to pick up Jasmine, he never would have dreamed that it would turn into an impromptu party. Not only had Dakota and Charon stopped by, but Nkosi and Prescott also turned up. Mycroft came with his mate, Boyd, and everyone was welcoming and friendly.

Warsaw hadn't felt such camaraderie since before Kennedy had died. Even better, he didn't have to watch what he said or hide the looks he wanted to give a man. He found it exceptionally liberating, even with a hint of bittersweetness to it.

When Urskin stood on the other side of the living space talking with Mycroft, Dakota noticed the way Warsaw was admiring his handsome mate. The friendly blond Komodo dragon shifter nudged his upper arm, getting his attention. He leaned close and sniffed at him, then winked as he straightened.

"Congrats, Warsaw," Dakota told him with a rakish grin. "When Urskin helped Charon, I ended up really likin' the guy, so I'm real glad that he ended up with an upstanding shifter like you."

Upstanding?

Warsaw couldn't help but frown at Dakota. "I was rogue," he pointed out, shaking his head. "Why would you call me upstanding?"

Dakota shrugged. "Eh, you made a bad call. Fell in with the wrong crowd." Patting him on his upper back, the enforcer continued, "But you pulled yourself out of it admirably. You got out, and Nkosi used that to our advantage."

Taking a slow sip of his beer, Warsaw processed that. He didn't feel like he'd done anything admirably. Instead of defecting and fighting against the rogues, Warsaw had sat out of the fight altogether.

"Look." Dakota rested his beer on his thigh as he leaned toward him from where he sat on the other side of the sofa. "I know Kennedy was like your brother." Dakota glanced toward the kitchenette where Miggs was pulling pastries out of the oven. Standing near his mate, was Delanrue, even as the large male spoke with Nkosi. "If Del or Dane asked me to do something, I can't imagine ever turning them down." Pinning him with a serious look, Dakota added, "And I sure as hell would never enter a fight against them. I'd be pulling my punches, which would make me a danger to everyone. Sitting out was the safest option."

As Warsaw nodded slowly, he still didn't think he deserved Dakota's consideration, but he wasn't going to contradict the man.

"Thank you," Warsaw decided to go with. "It's been . . . hard."

"Why didn't you tell me you were getting shit from that numbskull?" Nkosi demanded, stopping beside the sofa. "Lonnie doesn't have two brain cells to rub together, and his girlfriend should consider gagging him for the sake of saving us all from his moronic opinions."

Warsaw gaped at Nkosi, surprised to hear the vehemence in the man's words. "I, uh . . . well." He hadn't realized others shared his opinion of the man, but even if he had, he probably wouldn't have said anything. With a sigh, Warsaw mumbled, "It wasn't my place to comment on others. I just . . . I just want to finish out my restitution and move on with my life."

"And those assholes should have allowed you to do that without bother," Prescott declared, crossing his arms over his lean torso. He tapped the toe of his designer boot as he scowled at Warsaw. The eyeliner shaped his blue eyes to perfection, even though they were narrowed at him in clear disapproval. The wood duck shifter's skinny jeans hugged his long legs, and his shirt made the blue in his eyes pop. The guy looked like he'd just stepped off the page of a fashion magazine instead of having been doing some kind of filing for Mycroft all day. The pretty man scowled petulantly as he continued, "Not everyone can have a lily-white life like those jerks seem to think. Sometimes, people have to make tough choices."

"Life is shades of gray," Delanrue rumbled, moving toward them at Miggs's side, who was carrying a tray of goodies.

Warsaw grew nervous upon finding himself the center of

attention.

"And the gray on several of their auras is becoming increasingly dark." Urskin stopped behind the sofa and rested his hand on Warsaw's shoulder. He squeezed lightly, offering reassurance, as he let out a sigh. "Their thirst for vengeance at the loss of their friend is tarnishing them." Peering at Mycroft, Urskin stated, "I recommend counseling to help them move past their loss in a healthy way."

Mycroft wrapped his arms around Boyd from behind and rested his chin on his vampire's shoulder. He furrowed his brows as he nuzzled his lover. His expression clearly displayed how he thought that would go across — like a lead balloon.

"I wish I could order them into counseling," Mycroft began slowly, furrowing his brows. "But I can't order it on your say of the color of their auras." Lifting one hand from where he'd been rubbing Boyd's stomach, Mycroft quickly added, "And I do believe you, but singling them out would —"

"What if you didn't single them out?" Boyd asked, looking over his shoulder at Mycroft.

"What do you mean, baby?" Mycroft questioned.

Boyd swept his gaze around the group before resting his hands over Mycroft's wrists and meeting his gaze once more. "You and your people went through something horrible," he murmured, frowning. "So many of you lost friends and family to this . . . this . . . civil war between your kind." With a shrug, Boyd stated, "What about mandatory grief counseling for, well, everyone?"

"Oh, gods," Delanrue grumbled, glaring at Boyd. "You want us all to go to some shrink to talk about our *feelings*" — he curled his lip, clearly expressing what he thought of that — "because of a few assholes?"

Boyd's boy-next-door good looks took on a pinkish hue. "Well, uh . . . yeah."

Miggs tugged at Delanrue's arm, urging his mate to wrap it around his waist. Once the huge male had tucked his little guinea pig shifter close, Miggs peered way up at him and murmured, "It wouldn't be so bad. And think of all the people who are mourning in silence? It could help them."

Delanrue groaned, even as he grimaced and nodded. "Okay, baby."

Warsaw just managed to keep from gaping. Never in all his over a hundred years would he have thought the big bad council interrogator would fold like that. It seemed that if Delanrue's sweet mate wanted something, the burly Komodo dragon shifter did it.

Mycroft groaned softly as he pressed his forehead to Boyd's shoulder. "You're coming with me," he grumbled.

Boyd chuckled as he turned in Mycroft's arms. "Okay."

When the pair began exchanging soft kisses, Warsaw turned his attention to the others. He took in the groups' varying reactions. Some appeared resigned, a couple indifferent, and Prescott even snickered, as if he thought the idea was funny.

Nkosi scowled at Prescott. "Why does this amuse you, my mate?"

Prescott grinned broadly as he met Nkosi's annoyed gaze. "Ya'll are makin' it seem so horrible, but it's really not that bad." He shrugged as he continued, "I went to see Doc Digby for years before moving out here. If he can't come, maybe he'll have a recommendation for us."

Well, hell. Guess I'm going into therapy.

CHAPTER TEN

Urskin sat outside the office door, waiting for Warsaw to finish his session with Doctor Manson Killsie, the Shifter Council's new resident psychologist. The man was a green sea turtle shifter, and he'd come very highly recommended by Prescott's friend, Doctor Gordon Digby. Once Manson had agreed to work for the council, it had taken him almost a week to complete his move to Savannah.

During that time, Mycroft and his friends had used their connection with several councilmen to push through the mandate for everyone to meet with the doctor for grief counseling. The order went out that all shifters in the employ of the council were required to sit in a session with him at least three times. While the council couldn't force those not in their employ to see Manson, memos went out to everyone who'd taken part in the battle as well as to their families. They were encouraged to utilize Doctor Killsie's services, which would be free of charge to them.

From what Urskin had heard, many of the paranormals and humans alike had signed up for a session. So far, the doc had been extremely busy. The man was keeping long hours while he tried to meet with as many a day as possible. Still, Mycroft refused to allow him to work more than twelve, and Urskin understood why.

There was no sense in burning out the good doctor first thing.

As Warsaw's mate, Urskin had even had a session himself.

After around fifteen minutes of discussing Urskin's past, feelings, and plans for the future, Manson had smiled and told him, "When Warsaw's ready for you to join him, it'll be good to see you again." Then Urskin had learned that Manson was nearly as old as he was at just shy of three hundred years. For the rest of the session, they'd talked about the many changes they'd experienced as the decades rolled by them.

Urskin could see Manson becoming a good friend, if he ended up staying in the area after Warsaw finished his restitution to the council. As it was, they hadn't really talked about the future, yet. Instead, they kept their conversations low-key. While they slept together and shared meals together, they were still in the getting-to-know-you phase.

Most days, Urskin took care of Jasmine while Warsaw was at work. On the rare occasion that he couldn't take the sweet dog to an appointment with a client, he would leave her with Miggs. The guinea pig shifter adored the small beast, and Urskin guessed that a dog might soon end up being in Delanrue's future.

The office door opened, and Urskin lifted his attention from the western he'd been reading. He got an absolute kick out of the way so many authors romanticized cowboys and the old west. Having lived through the time period, Urskin knew better.

Cowboys were not clean, they were not respectable, and they didn't save the day.

Okay, so I ran across a few that were different, willing to do the right thing, but most of them . . . not so much.

Closing the app on his phone, Urskin rose to his feet. He shoved the device into his pocket as he took in Warsaw's drawn expression. His lover appeared a little pale, and his eyes held a telltale redness that Urskin understood.

My poor familiar ended up crying at some point.

Urskin would never draw attention to that knowledge, however. Instead, he offered Manson a small smile before resting a hand on Warsaw's upper arm. After a light squeeze, he touched Warsaw's jaw with his free hand, gaining his attention.

Warsaw's smile appeared sad, but it was there, so Urskin took it as a win.

"I'll see you next week, Warsaw," Manson stated quietly. "Same time."

"Okay, Doc," Warsaw replied without taking his gaze away from Urskin. His next words were for him. "Let's go."

Urskin nodded, taking a step back and pivoting. Sliding his hand down Warsaw's arm, he teased his fingertips along his familiar's before releasing him. As they walked, the backs of their hands bumped.

In the privacy of their suite, Warsaw was often quite affectionate, even when they weren't having sex, resting a hand on his leg, squeezing his fingers, and teasing the hairs at Urskin's nape. Outside their space, however, Warsaw still struggled to connect. That was why a surge of surprise flooded Urskin when Warsaw threaded his fingers through Urskin's and held on.

Glancing at Warsaw, Urskin noticed the clench of his lover's jaw. He wondered if this was an assignment instigated by Manson, but he didn't question Warsaw on it. Instead, Urskin squeezed lightly in silent encouragement.

After a moment of silence, Warsaw asked, "Where's Jasmine?"

That it had taken so long for Warsaw to ask about his beloved Shih Tzu told Urskin exactly how stuck in his head he was.

"Ten minutes into your session, Charon came and whisked her away," Urskin told his familiar. "He picked up a new set of bows and a tennis ball. He said he was going to take her to the south community area to play fetch."

The south community area was just off the dining hall. The

place was open, had dozens of outdoor tables, and was well monitored. There was nowhere for anyone to sneak up on the sweet girl without there being plenty of warning.

Jasmine was safe there.

Warsaw nodded. "Okay."

"Do you want to go pick her up?" Urskin asked, offering his familiar's hand another light squeeze. "We could play fetch with her, too."

After a few seconds of hesitation, Warsaw nodded. "Yeah." He paused in the hallway, glancing left and right at the junction they were at. Then Warsaw lifted his free hand and cradled Urskin's jaw. His blond brows were furrowed, and his attention appeared riveted on Urskin's mouth. "Thanks for your patience."

Before Urskin could come up with a response, Warsaw dipped his head and pressed his lips to Urskin's own. Just like every time he felt his familiar's mouth on him, his heart took to racing in his chest. Urskin's blood fired in his veins, and his gut clenched with need.

Only the knowledge of where they stood kept Urskin from wrapping his arms around Warsaw and pressing against him tightly. Instead, he gripped his shifter's upper arms for balance as he opened for the other man's questing tongue. Urskin relished the taste of his familiar, the other half of his soul, as Warsaw ravished his mouth.

Just as quickly as the kiss began, Warsaw ended it. He lifted his head and peered down at him with hungry eyes. After pinching his kiss-swollen lips together in a hard line as he took a noisy breath, he blew it out through pursed lips.

"Every time I see you, I wanna do that," Warsaw told him gruffly. He glanced up and down the halls again before refocusing on him. "But I'm not brave enough yet."

Understanding dawned on Urskin, and he smiled at Warsaw. "I'm not going anywhere, and neither are you," he stated confidently. "Even if you never grow comfortable enough to kiss me in front of others, all that matters is that I know you'd like to someday."

Warsaw blinked at him before jerking a nod. "Yeah. That. Thanks." Then he slid his hand up to scratch lightly at Urskin's scalp. "Like the feel of your hair." He finished the move by sliding his fingertips down Urskin's sideburns and along his goatee. Lowering his hand, Warsaw rumbled, "Different than mine."

Urskin smiled up at Warsaw. "I like that you like it." He didn't fight it when his lover turned and began walking again. "And for the record," he continued softly. "I like your hair, too."

With Urskin having joined Warsaw living at Shifter Headquarters, they'd been given a larger, nicer suite. The place had a large jetted tub. After a long day, one of their favorite ways to relax in the evening was to lounge together in the water.

Most wouldn't think it, but Warsaw enjoyed being the little spoon. Urskin would recline against the back of the tub with Warsaw resting against his chest. Sometimes they would share their days. Sometimes they would sit quietly and listen to the jets. Urskin would read, and Warsaw would doze while he petted his hard chest and abdominals as well as his hair and scalp.

Jasmine even had a bed on a platform next to the tub, so she could hang out with them.

Of course, that limited the amount of sex that happened in there, but Urskin didn't mind. They had plenty of that as it was. On a daily basis, Urskin utilized a healing cream for his ass, so he never ran the risk of being sore or getting torn by his shifter's massive rod.

Urskin's absolute favorite times, however, were when Jasmine got bored and decided to find something to do in another area of the suite. He would take complete advantage of their alone time and play with Warsaw's body, ringing as much pleasure as possible from him. His familiar loved a finger in his ass, and his nipples were a true hot spot. Urskin had thought about trying to convince Warsaw to get them pierced.

Maybe someday.

Reaching a side door, Warsaw led the way outside. He continued to hold Urskin's hand as they rounded the building. Warsaw didn't even release him when they entered the outdoor community area.

Urskin quickly spotted Charon, Miggs, Prescott, and Nkosi relaxing on the far side. The foursome was talking and laughing. Well, the first three were, anyway. Nkosi kept panning his gaze over the area as if assessing for threats.

As Urskin watched, he spotted Jasmine bounding back to the table. Her long brown hair had been gathered into two pigtails above her ears, keeping her hair out of her face. There were red, glittery bows attached to each hair band.

Smiling, Urskin found her adorable as she bounced in place, her tongue hanging out, clearly waiting for the ball she'd dropped as Charon's feet to be tossed again.

She's going to be worn out tonight.

"Fucking asshole."

Upon hearing the female voice, Urskin snapped his attention to the left. Red hair caught his peripheral. He peered over his shoulder and spotted Rita, but she quickly slipped into the dining hall.

Urskin bit back a growl, but Warsaw's hold propelled him forward, returning his attention to his man.

Due to the fact that Richmond was a shifter enforcer, he'd done as instructed and gone to see Doctor Killsie. Urskin knew Richmond repeatedly went because Mycroft needed their appointment schedule so he could work their assignments around them . . . and Mycroft told him. Urskin also knew that Richmond had taken his mate with him at one point. Lonnie was under review for attacking them, so he'd been forced to go. As Rita wasn't an employee of the council, they couldn't force her, and she'd flat-out refused . . . loudly.

Others had overheard Rita calling it a weak human practice that was beneath her.

Urskin knew there was one more that Damian had been close friends with—another lion shifter named Priest. The big male was a tracker and still out on assignment. Occasionally, he wondered what the guy would think about the new, required policy and if he would capitulate.

Time will tell.

In the meantime, Urskin would do his best to help Warsaw heal.

"Hey, guys," Miggs greeted with a grin. "Pull up a chair." He pointed at the cupcakes on the table. "Cupcake? They're lemon meringue."

Warsaw grunted and quickly took a seat. "Thanks." He finally released Urskin in his hurry to grab one.

Urskin chuckled softly, not at all offended. While Miggs was an amazing baker, that wasn't it. Miggs knew lemon meringue was Warsaw's favorite. Urskin cast a warm smile the guinea pig shifter's way in silent thanks for his thoughtfulness. Then he grabbed one of the tasty treats for himself.

Charon threw the ball again, but Jasmine ignored it. Instead, the little cutie yipped excitedly in greeting as she raced to Warsaw. His lover bent and picked his darling up with one hand and set her on his lap, continuing to stuff a cupcake into his mouth without missing a beat.

The group chuckled—even Nkosi—and Warsaw's lips curved into a wry, frosting-covered smile.

As Urskin chewed his own bite, sitting back and enjoying the sun, he smiled fondly at Warsaw. When his familiar's blue-eyed gaze landed on him and the shifter smiled back at him before turning and grabbing his third cupcake, Urskin felt his stomach clench. The unmistakable sensation of butterflies in his belly assaulted him.

Urskin knew that feeling. He'd felt it before . . . many years before.

I'm falling in love with my familiar.

As Urskin relaxed with their friends, he knew that was how it should be. He would love the buffalo shifter until the day they died. Considering Warsaw was less than a hundred and fifty and could live for a few more centuries, Urskin knew that would be for a very long time, barring injury.

And I'll never allow that to happen.

Movement to his left caught Urskin's attention, and he spotted Rita half-hidden behind a decorative shrub. She spoke with a huge black man with penetrating black eyes and a scowl on his face. The man had his arms crossed over his expansive torso as he tipped his bald head down to listen to whatever she was saying.

Urskin's stomach churned once more, this time from discomfort. His magick slithered just under his skin, reacting to his unease. He took a slow deep breath to settle himself.

Tapping the tip of his foot against Nkosi's heel, Urskin drew the black mamba shifter's attention. "Who's that?" he murmured, tipping his chin ever-so-subtly in the pair's direction.

Nkosi glanced just as furtively. Then he focused on where Jasmine was licking frosting off of Warsaw's face. "That's Priest," the snake shifter stated. "Must be back from assignment."

Huh. Things just got a whole lot more interesting.

CHAPTER ELEVEN

Warsaw stood in the doorway to his bedroom, naked and nervous. Urskin already sat in bed, naked to the waist, wearing only a pair of lounging pants. His fingers twitched with his desire to touch as arousal poured heat through his veins, and his dick swelled.

After licking his lips, Warsaw cleared his throat. His lover lifted his chin, pausing his reading of whatever was on his tablet. Warsaw knew that Urskin loved to read, and he appreciated that the warlock always seemed to drop everything when Warsaw asked him to.

Urskin's dark eyes narrowed as he swept his gaze over Warsaw's naked form. His dark lips curved into a warm, hungry smile. Placing his tablet aside, he held out that hand, palm up, in invitation.

As much as Warsaw wanted to go to Urskin, he lingered in the doorway.

Cocking his head to the side, Urskin slowly lowered his hand. "Something on your mind, Warsaw?"

Warsaw jerked a nod. Rubbing the back of his neck for a few seconds, he tried to find the right words. Even his nerves didn't deflate his erection, and Warsaw felt a mixture of anticipation and butterflies.

I know he'll agree. I just need to get the words out.

Lowering his hand, Warsaw clenched both into fists. "Will you fuck me?" he blurted out, his focus fixed firmly on the foot of the bed.

"No."

Jerking his attention to Urskin's face, Warsaw stared into his mate's serene black eyes. For a few seconds, he couldn't believe what he'd heard. "What?"

Urskin's dark lips curved into a small smile, and his eyes glittered in the bedroom light. "No, I will not fuck you," he answered, clear and concise.

Warsaw felt his cheeks heat in embarrassment, and that did start to wilt his erection.

Lifting his hand again, Urskin once again beckoned to him, but Warsaw couldn't get his feet to move.

"Come here, Warsaw," Urskin encouraged, wiggling his fingers. "Come here, my familiar." When Warsaw still couldn't get himself to move, Urskin told him, "I'll not fuck you, but I would very much like to make love to you."

Snapping his attention back to Urskin's face, Warsaw took in the warm, welcoming smile on his lips. His expression held a wealth of reassurance and understanding. Even his eyes seemed to gleam with heat and need as he held Warsaw's gaze.

"Come to me, Warsaw," Urskin encouraged again. "Come to me and let me make you fly."

Warsaw sucked in a quick breath. A fresh wave of excitement burned through him, heating him from the inside out. His erection roared back to life.

Managing to get his feet unstuck from the floor, Warsaw crossed the room. He reached out and took Urskin's hand. He should have known better than to doubt his mate. After all, Urskin always took care of him, in every interaction.

While Warsaw was the larger of them, Urskin was definitely the more dominant . . . even if up until then, Warsaw had been the one topping.

Now, I want to change that.

Warsaw loved the feel of Urskin's fingers in him, playing with his anus, massaging his chute muscles. He wanted to know what it would be like to submit to his mate . . . in all ways. His channel clenched and released as he watched Urskin slide from the bed, his anticipation ramping up.

While Warsaw had thought it was the most difficult thing to admit in all the world, he'd talked to his therapist about ass fucking. He'd explained his fears. Then Manson had asked if he believed Urskin would ease all those doubts if he only asked. In that moment, Warsaw knew that the only thing to fear was his own inhibitions.

My mate will take care of everything.

As Warsaw watched, Urskin pushed down his pants with his free hand. He shoved the comforter down next. Then he guided Warsaw onto the bed, and he lay on his stomach. After giving Warsaw's hand a squeeze, Urskin released him.

"Soooo," Urskin crooned, drawing the word out softly. "I've dreamed of this moment since I met you, Warsaw, since I realized you were my familiar." Urskin's smile held a mixture of hunger and trepidation. "And I don't want to hurt you for the world." Settling on the bed beside Warsaw, Urskin rubbed a hand down his broad back. "If I do anything you don't like, please, tell me instantly, and I'll stop."

Warsaw felt his nerves ease, and he relaxed on the sheet. "I trust you," Warsaw whispered. "I know whatever you do will feel amazing." When Urskin opened his mouth, his concern still evident in his dark eyes, Warsaw reached over and gripped his wrist. "But you have my word. If I don't like something, I'll tell you."

Urskin relaxed, the tension leaving his lean shoulders. "Good."

Rising onto his knees, Urskin leaned over and grabbed the lube from the nightstand. Instead of popping it open and pouring some onto his hand, he set it next to Warsaw's hip. Then he swung a leg over and rested a knee on each side of his thighs.

For the first time in his life, Warsaw felt a man's erection tap against his backside. He couldn't help it. Instinct had him clenching.

"Easy, Warsaw," Urskin crooned softly. Lowering his torso, he pressed a kiss to Warsaw's shoulder. "Let me help you relax."

"Okay." Warsaw felt a smidge embarrassed that his voice came out so strained, especially when he knew he wanted this so badly. After blowing out a slow breath, Warsaw murmured, "I trust you, Urskin."

After pressing another kiss to Warsaw's shoulder, Urskin murmured, "I'm honored by your gift." Then he straightened a little. "Okay. This is a spell I learned from an angel a century back. Let's see if I get it right."

Warsaw peered over his shoulder, watching. He saw Urskin cup his palm and close his eyes. His mate whispered something in a language that Warsaw couldn't hope to understand, and a warm, golden glow encompassed Urskin's hand.

A second later, the glow faded, and Urskin grinned, clearly pleased with himself. He pressed his hands together, and something squished between his palms, oozing between his fingers. When Urskin caught Warsaw looking, he winked at him.

"This is lotion from the bottle in the bathroom," Urskin told him. When Warsaw opened his mouth to ask how, his mate beat him to it. "I ran into an angel some time ago and did the male a favor. He repaid me by teaching me a transportation spell." With a shrug, Urskin explained, "I can't use it for moving anything large, but for small items like a handful of lotion, it's perfect."

Before Warsaw could ask questions—like what had Urskin helped the angel with—his mate lowered his palms to Warsaw's upper back and began to knead his muscles. Warsaw let out a low moan as he collapsed back to the sheet. His body felt as if it might melt beneath Urskin's ministrations.

While Urskin had gently massaged Warsaw in the tub on many occasions, it had never felt like this. His mate made a point of finding every knot, every twinge, and every tight spot, and he eased them all. His fingers were magick, and he wasn't uttering a single spell.

Soon enough, Warsaw felt as if his body had been turned to mush. His mind floated pleasantly, and he began to doze. Warsaw felt Urskin's ministrations change subtly as he began working one hand down his spine. The massage to his hips drew a sigh from him, and he barely noticed Urskin begin teasing his fingertips along the top of his trench.

The sound of the lube opening pulled Warsaw from his relaxed floaty headspace, but only by a little. The teasing down his crack tugged at him a bit more. However, the warm tingles created by Urskin working that sensitive bit of skin lulled him once more.

Finally, Urskin easing his knees between Warsaw's thighs and urging them wider truly brought him back to the surface. He was too relaxed to tense, though. Plus, the slick finger playing with his anus caused warmth to churn in his gut.

Never would Warsaw have expected it, as he'd never dared to touch himself there, but the feel of his most intimate muscles being manipulated felt so damn fantastic.

"More," Warsaw found himself pleading when Urskin danced over and around his muscle again and again. "Please."

"Anything you want, Warsaw," Urskin assured.

Then Urskin eased the tip of his finger past the guardian muscle, breaching him.

Warsaw groaned softly, his body accepting the intrusion easily. The feel of Urskin moving his finger along the sensitive muscles of his chute caused his groin to heat. When a second finger eased in beside the first, his balls began to feel heavy.

On instinct, Warsaw widened his thighs. His cock ached,

and he began rocking into those touches. Between them and the feel of the sheet sliding along his erection, Warsaw began to float with the pleasure of it. He felt his balls begin to pull tight, and he groaned, his body flashing hot as sweat broke out on his skin.

"Ursk," Warsaw whined. "C-Close."

"Good," Urskin crooned into his ear. "But not enough. I want you soaring."

As if to facilitate that, Urskin slid his fingers over that special spot inside Warsaw. Zings of hot pleasure erupted within him. His body jolted with the intensity, and Warsaw groaned.

Unable to control himself, Warsaw jerked his hips. He rutted into the blanket over and over. Each time he came back, those fingers were there, massaging over his prostate.

Then Warsaw was there. Just as Urskin had promised, he was soaring. His senses reeled, his eyes threatened to roll back in his head, and he shuddered as hard jolts of ecstasy surged through him.

Bliss. How did I ever live without this?

Even as Warsaw continued to come, his release pulsing through him, he felt Urskin ease his fingers from him, and he whined in displeasure. A second later, he felt something else push into him. It felt bigger, longer, and stretched him in a way that felt so very right.

"Oh!" Warsaw gasped, shivering as delightful sensations lit up his nerve endings the deeper Urskin pushed into him. "Ursk!"

"Relax, Warsaw," Urskin purred into his ear. He rubbed his palm up and down Warsaw's side. "It'll be better soon. Just take a few deep breaths."

Through Warsaw's pleasure-bleached brain, he realized his mate completely misunderstood. "No," he whispered. "No, I—"

"Gods, I'm sorry, baby," Urskin muttered as he began to pull out. "I didn't mean—"

"Fuck." Warsaw was botching it up. Swinging a hand back, he grabbed Urskin's hip in a tight hold, not allowing him to move further away. "Stop."

Urskin paused, his hips freezing. He continued to skate his right hand up and down Warsaw's side, while keeping his weight on his left hand where he levered over him. Lowering a little, Urskin pressed wet, nuzzling kisses to his nape.

"Talk to me, Warsaw," Urskin pleaded, his voice tight with unmistakable need. "Tell me what you need."

Turning his head, Warsaw met Urskin's gaze. He saw the internal struggle being waged within those black depths. Needing to ease Urskin as much as he needed to be fucked, Warsaw smiled up at his mate.

"I just need you, Urskin," Warsaw told him. He slowly clenched his chute muscles around his mate's half-embedded dick. "Don't need you to wait until I adjust. You feel amazing." Seeing Urskin's wide nostrils flair and a muscle tick in his jaw, Warsaw did it again. "Please, my mate. Please fuck me."

Urskin groaned around a feral-looking smile. "Not fucking you, my familiar," he reminded. Then he pushed back into Warsaw's body in one long, slow glide. Sprawling along Warsaw's larger body, Urskin rested his weight on him. "Loving you."

Then Urskin began to move. He eased his prick partway out, only to snap it forward again. He sped up his strokes as he adjusted his angle.

The second Urskin nailed his prostate, Warsaw cried out with the sparking pleasure of it. His chute's nerve endings flared up with delicious tingles. He shuddered with delight as he moaned Urskin's name over and over as his mate pegged his gland again and again.

Warsaw reveled in the sensation of Urskin's dick sliding across his inner walls, setting those nerve endings on fire. His cock throbbed anew, never softening. Arching his back, he managed to get his knees under him a little, and he began pushing back into each of Urskin's ruts.

Urskin's growl set Warsaw's blood on fire. The way his groin smacked the skin of his ass caused the hairs on his thighs to stand on end. The feel of Urskin's lean sweaty body sliding against his own made him feel as if he'd never been closer to the man riding his ass.

"Come for me," Urskin encouraged, nailing his gland over and over. "Squeeze my dick, my familiar."

Gasping, Warsaw feared he wasn't quite close enough for a second orgasm.

Then Urskin reached under him and gripped his nipple. He squeezed and twisted just right. The pleasure-pain zinged straight to his balls.

Warsaw's orgasm welled up within him. His cock erupted, and he poured his release into the sheets beneath him. His body jolted and shuddered as his senses sang, and his mind fuzzed out from the ecstasy of the best sex of his life.

His trembling limbs gave way, and Warsaw collapsed to the bed as he moaned Urskin's name.

"Gods, that's a beautiful sound, Warsaw," Urskin mumbled, his warm breath ghosting over the damp skin of his back. "So fucking good."

When Urskin began to move, to ease off his back, Warsaw reached back once more. He gripped his lover again, stilling his movements. "Stay still," he urged, squeezing his mate's hip lightly. Even feeling his body flush for a different reason, Warsaw forced himself to admit, "I like feeling you . . . like this. Feeling you . . . inside me."

Urskin relaxed onto his back, pressing light kisses to his skin. "I think . . ." He hesitated a second, then continued, "I think, you may be a natural bottom."

Warsaw thought about that for a few seconds, how he felt

about it. "As long as it's you." Then he squeezed Urskin's hip once more before bringing his arm back around to rest it beside his head. "I'm okay with that."

"My amazing familiar," Urskin whispered, licking at his skin. "So perfect. Perfect for me." He rubbed up and down Warsaw's skin, teasing his flesh. "Thank you."

"No, thank you," Warsaw countered. "I—" Then he grimaced as the chill of the sheets finally began to register. "And as much as I'd love to stay just like this, I guess I don't want to after all."

"Oh?" Urskin lifted away from him, pushing up with his arms. "You feeling okay?" As he asked, he moved to the side and rubbed a hand over Warsaw's back.

Warsaw nodded, rolling and giving Urskin a wry grin. "I'm in the wet spot."

Urskin tipped his head back and laughed. Then he scooted out of bed and held out his hand. "Come on, my familiar. I'll wash your back."

Warsaw took Urskin's hand, surprised to find his legs a little unsteady, and together they made their way to the bathroom.

A couple of minutes later, their shower together was interrupted by a pounding knock on their door.

Warsaw wrapped a towel around his waist, unmindful of his dripping on the floor. Reaching the door, he noticed Urskin following. His warlock stood by the trench coat he wore. Urskin had explained to him once that it had many, many hidden pockets.

Refocusing on the door, Warsaw pulled it open. A second later, he wished he'd hollered through the door first.

Priest stood on the other side. Scowling, the huge male used a big palm to shove open the door, and he stalked inside. Just as quickly, he shut the door behind him.

Warsaw readied for Priest's attack, and he saw that Urskin had done the same. His warlock held some sort of powder in his hand. All semblance of afterglow was forgotten.

"Heard you'd found your mate." Priest glanced between them. "Congrats." As Warsaw's jaw sagged open, shock flooding him, Priest continued, "Rita means to kill you and your dog tomorrow." The huge male crossed his arms over his chest. "Thought you oughta know."

CHAPTER TWELVE

U rskin hated the plan. Still, the prior evening, he hadn't
been able to come up with a better one.

As soon as Priest had made his announcement, he'd begun
to turn to leave.

"Hold it," Urskin had ordered, anger and fear swirling
through him. "You need to tell us more." Then he'd held up
his cell phone—which had been tucked inside a pocket of his
trench coat—and had added, "I have Mycroft on the line. He's
on his way."

Priest had tipped his head back and heaved a deep sigh.
"Fine." Then he'd stalked to the sofa and plopped onto it
without invitation. "Gimme a beer, would ya, man?" He'd
glanced at Warsaw, letting him know who he was talking to.

Then, to Urskin's continued shock, Priest had begun talking to Jasmine, who'd immediately hopped onto the sofa and
sprawled on his lap, legs in the air, exposing her belly, eager
for pets.

Warsaw had gotten Priest a beer.

Urskin still had a hard time reconciling that image. The
huge bruiser of a man had been so gentle and, well, cute with
Warsaw's dog. Still, Urskin trusted the sweet animal's instincts. Priest wasn't a threat to them.

After Mycroft had arrived, the head enforcer had asked
Priest for specifics. The large tracker had explained everything Rita had told him. Of course, most of that had just been

a long, boring rant about how Warsaw needed to be punished further for his crimes. She wanted his little rat dog dead because that would hurt him even more than death.

According to Rita, Jasmine was the only creature on the earth that Warsaw loved, so he needed to lose it before being killed.

Urskin had felt his gut clench when Warsaw hadn't countered what Priest repeated. He'd done his best to push the feeling down, especially after his familiar had given himself to him. Urskin knew that Warsaw would be a tough nut to crack, and he would be patient.

I have all the time in the world.

Or I will, as soon as this bitch is taken care of.

As normal, Warsaw had headed to work. He'd received his orders from the leader of the grounds crew. Warsaw had been tasked with hiking the area and gathering up feathers lost by the large flocks of wild turkeys that roamed the area.

That meant Warsaw would have to hike all over the dozens of acres, and Rita could plan her attack anywhere. Too bad Priest hadn't known where she planned. He'd explained that when he realized her intention, he'd bluntly told her, "I'm not available to help you tomorrow."

Considering Priest intended to thwart her plans, his words had been completely true, so Rita had just huffed and stomped off.

"Try to relax," Delanrue encouraged, resting his hand on Urskin's shoulder. "Warsaw will be fine. We'll make certain of it."

Urskin nodded. After all, no other outcome was acceptable.

"Besides," Delanrue continued, his voice taking on a growl. "Dakota and Charon are the ones taking Jasmine for a walk, and Rita wants to kill the dog first." He snorted. "Dumb broad."

Again, Urskin nodded. He knew that Dakota would keep his mate and the dog safe, but that didn't mean Rita wouldn't change her plans.

Or maybe she has a plan to get Jasmine away from them.

Shaking his head, Urskin reminded himself not to borrow trouble. He began strolling through the gardens, needing to get his feet moving. Standing still would just drive him crazy.

"Hey, come with me." Delanrue beckoned to him. "I have an idea of how to keep your mind off everything."

Urskin couldn't imagine what could possibly accomplish that, but he obeyed. He followed Delanrue through a maze of hedges. From the position of the sun, he knew they were rounding the building.

After nearly ten minutes, Urskin was damn tempted to tease, "Are we there yet?"

Except, then Urskin spotted the dying willow and knew that had to be the destination. Seeing the brown spots here and there on the bark, Urskin could make a good guess as to the cause. He shook his head sadly, hoping the fungal rot hadn't yet set too deeply into the tree's roots, or he would have no shot at rejuvenating it.

"Think you can save it?" Delanrue asked, sounding more curious than worried.

Urskin knew it was more busy work than anything else. Still, he answered, "Maybe," and got to work.

Several hours, several spells, and after plenty more hiking to find certain natural ingredients from the environment, Urskin cast the final spell. Once he was finished, he could already see the tree's improvement. The willow's leaves were more vibrant, the sagging branches held more vitality, and even a bird sang from one of its branches.

Urskin peered up at his handiwork and smiled. He would monitor it for the next couple of months. If he caught any other problems, he would correct them.

I suppose I'll also walk the grounds and see if I can help any other plants.

With him staying in one place, Urskin had to be careful how he advertised his skills. He didn't want any sort of reputation as a miracle worker or holy man getting out. That would just draw attention to himself, and he couldn't leave until Warsaw's restitution was done.

And I've convinced him to travel with me.

So far, Urskin had been hesitant to bring it up.

Maybe after this business with Rita is done.

"Del, we have a problem." Dakota's voice came over the walkie-talkie he carried.

"Go ahead," Delanrue ordered.

"We lost Jasmine." That was Charon, and he sounded so damn contrite.

That didn't stop Urskin from snarling, "What? How?"

Good thing Urskin wasn't the one who had the device.

Delanrue narrowed his eyes at Urskin as he ordered, "Where are you? Tell me what happened."

"We're in the south gardens," Dakota revealed, and they both started jogging in that direction. Del's brother's voice continued to come over the speaker. "We rounded a corner, and Jasmine stopped dead. When we encouraged her forward, she whined and started wriggling to get away." With a groan, Dakota admitted, "We didn't get to her fast enough. Jasmine tugged her collar over her head and took off. We're doing our best to follow her scent trail, and if I had to guess, I think she's trying to find Warsaw."

Warsaw.

Urskin slid to a stop. Closing his eyes, he reached out with his magick. Instantly, his power showed him which way to go.

"Urskin?"

Spinning, Urskin told Delanrue, "This way."

Then Urskin started running. He ducked under tree branches, skittered around bushes, and leaped over downed branches. Urskin made his way as swiftly as possible, following his magick's connection to his familiar.

Urskin heard them before he saw them.

Jasmine was yelping, not in pain, but in fear. Warsaw's low growl was unmistakable. It was Rita's laughter that really put his teeth on edge.

"He's such a pussy for this little rat dog." Lonnie's unmistakable sneer-filled voice sounded through the air. "I can't wait to see you cry when we snap the little beast's neck."

Breaking through some branches, Urskin skidded to a stop and took in the scene. Warsaw gripped the shoulder strap of the pouch he wore for collecting feathers. He stared daggers at Lonnie, a thunderous expression on his flushed face.

To Urskin's surprise, Rita held Jasmine, who was crying in fear and wriggling to get away . . . because Gretchen was slowly approaching, a malicious gleam in her blue eyes.

"Ohhh, look at the fear in the rat's eyes," Gretchen crooned sadistically. "Gods, such a beautiful look. Glad I didn't kill it the first time. So worth the extra trouble."

"*You* hurt her?" Warsaw growled, his blue eyes narrowing further. "You bitch. You'd hurt a defenseless dog just to get at me?"

Gretchen shrugged her slender shoulder negligently. "Of course."

"But we smelled cat," Warsaw muttered, revealing his confusion. "And there were claw marks."

Gretchen held up her right hand and wiggled her gloved fingers, showing off the claws attached to the fabric. "Cat piss," she stated with a cold grin. "Great for hiding true scent." Stopping next to Rita, Gretchen reached for the animal. "Give it here."

"No." Rita pulled Jasmine further away from Gretchen. "You botched it up last time." With a curl of her lip, Rita ignored her friend's angry expression as she turned to look at

Warsaw. "But I'm glad you did, too. Now I get to watch first hand."

As Rita spoke, she slid her hand around Jasmine's neck.

Urskin swung his arms like a windmill as he chanted swiftly.

"Stop him," Lonnie ordered, pointing at him. Although, Urskin noticed the coward didn't take a step toward him.

The wind kicked up, buffeting Rita and Gretchen with great gusts. It caught the nearby willow branches, causing them to swing to and fro. The fronds smacked against the women, making them stagger.

Rita lost her grip on Jasmine. The little dog tumbled to the ground.

Instantly, Urskin cut the power to his spell, knowing Jasmine would have no chance of moving against the strength of his winds.

The women lunged at Jasmine, but the dog was too quick. Jasmine streaked between their legs, racing toward Warsaw. Rita shifted, transforming into a large tiger, and she took off after Jasmine.

Warsaw's body grew, his clothes tearing from his expanding form. In seconds, he lowered his massive buffalo's head and bellowed in anger while pawing the ground. To Urskin's surprise, Jasmine ran right between Warsaw's legs without fear, skidding to stop to cower behind him.

Rita lunged, attacking.

"Shit," Gretchen hissed. Pointing, she shouted, "Help her, Lonnie."

Shaking his head, Lonnie kept his attention pinned on Delanrue, who'd circled the clearing to come out behind them. A second later, Dakota appeared with Charon.

"Fuck!" Gretchen shifted, turning into a long-legged gazelle. She immediately began bounding away between the trees.

Casting another spell, Urskin took control of the willow's limbs. He waved his hands in the air, curling his fingers and spinning his wrists. In response, the bendy branches wound around Gretchen's horns, legs, and body, ceasing her flight.

As Gretchen struggled, jumping, bucking, and rearing, trying to break free, Urskin winced. He mentally apologized to the tree and swore that he would return to mend anything his actions had broken on it. Gretchen froze, and Urskin saw why.

Priest and Richmond strode from between the trees. The black man glowered at the group, a dark frown turning down his lips. The pain filling Richmond's brown eyes as he stared at Gretchen caused Urskin's breath to catch in his throat.

"I'm sorry, Rich," Priest rumbled, shaking his head. "I didn't know she was involved."

Richmond sighed deeply as he swallowed roughly. "I should have, though," he muttered, his voice breaking.

Gretchen returned to human form. "Richmond," she cried pleadingly. "I can explain."

"Don't talk to me," Richmond ordered, turning away from her. "We're done. I'll have our mate-bond dissolved at once."

"No!" Gretchen screamed, nearly managing to slip from the branches in her smaller form. "You bastard!"

Ignoring Gretchen's screeches, Richmond disappeared back between the trees.

"Whoa, Lonnie." Priest clamped a huge hand on his probably ex-friend's shoulder. "You're not going anywhere. You're under arrest."

The yowl of a cat in pain snapped Urskin's attention away from the unfolding drama. He gaped, shocked at what he saw. Somehow, Warsaw had managed to corner Rita against a tree trunk. From Rita's position, it looked like she'd tried to leap away, but Warsaw had caught her and skewered her with his horns, pinning her to the tree. Blood poured from

Rita's wounds as she tried to slash her claws through Warsaw's buffalo's thick hair. While the occasional blood pooled up, the buffalo didn't move, holding steady.

After a moment, Rita's movements slowed, then stopped altogether, and she hung limply against the tree, caught by the buffalo's horns.

Enforcer Delanrue approached Warsaw. "That'll do, War," he rumbled, patting his large shoulder. "I'll take her body."

Warsaw stayed still for several heartbeats, and Urskin moved toward his lover's buffalo. Keeping in mind that his familiar was cognizant in animal form—hell, several times Urskin had watched Warsaw's buffalo frolic with Jasmine while he'd communed with nature—he took Delanrue's place. He rubbed his hands over Warsaw's thick fur soothingly.

"It's fine, my familiar," Urskin murmured to his lover. "Jasmine is safe now. You're safe now. Put Rita's body down."

Huffing deeply, Warsaw eased back a few steps. He shook his head, dumping the tiger from his thick horns. After a few more pets, Urskin felt the telltale shudder of his lover's shift begin.

Urskin took a step backward and quickly shucked his trench coat. Spreading it over Warsaw's shoulders as soon as he'd returned to his human form, he hugged his shifter's wide frame. A second later, Jasmine joined them, wriggling onto his lover's lap. When Urskin knelt, the dog licked his face just as much as Warsaw's, and he couldn't help but smile.

Warsaw finally tipped his head back and cradled Urskin's jaw. "You okay?" he asked gruffly.

"I'm fine, Warsaw," Urskin assured, turning his head to quickly kiss his lover's palm. "They didn't even get close to me." Sweeping his gaze over Warsaw's partially covered frame, he spotted the healing scratches on his neck and face.

Urskin touched around them lightly and asked, "What about you?"

"I'm just fine, my mate," Warsaw assured. Then he slipped his hold around to grip Urskin's nape. "Come'ere."

Urskin obeyed, opening easily when Warsaw sealed their mouths together. He welcomed his shifter's probing tongue, suckling on it lightly before teasing his own along it. Humming, enjoying Warsaw's unique flavor, Urskin met his lover thrust for thrust.

A low chuckle followed by the clearing of a throat broke them up.

Dakota grinned as he carried a trussed and gagged Gretchen from the clearing. Delanrue, who was staring around the clearing with his arms crossed, was probably the one who'd cleared his throat.

As Priest pushed Lonnie before him, following Dakota, Lonnie snarled, "You were my friend, dick. What the hell?"

Priest snorted. "Yeah, well, every group of friends has to have one moron in it, and I always knew you were it."

Mycroft blew out a breath as he shook his head. "I swear. We clear up one group of haters only to be infected by another." With a roll of his eyes, he focused on Warsaw. "Your restitution is fulfilled, Warsaw. I had it processed last night after we learned of Rita's impending attack." Mycroft held out an envelope. "Your official pardon is inside. I have one on file, too."

"Thank you, sir," Warsaw rumbled, taking the envelope.

"You're welcome, and I'm sorry for the trouble," Mycroft told him. Resting his hands on his hips, he asked, "What are you going to do now?"

Warsaw glanced at Urskin before meeting Mycroft's gaze again. "I'm not sure. We haven't talked about it." His cheeks took on a hint of pink as he added, "Thought we'd have a little more time."

"Well, good luck to you, Warsaw." With that, Mycroft headed into the trees.

Delanrue patted Warsaw on the shoulder. "Don't be a stranger, War." Then he followed the head enforcer.

Urskin sat on the ground beside Warsaw, seeing the troubled furrowing of his brows. "What's wrong?"

Warsaw snapped his attention to Urskin. "Nothing." He scoffed quietly as his lips curved into a wide smile. "Not a damn thing is wrong." Then Warsaw sobered. "But I do have to clear up one thing."

"What's that?"

"Rita claimed that Jasmine was the only thing I loved in this world, but that's not true." Warsaw gripped Urskin's hand, threading their fingers together. "I love you, too, Urskin. I just didn't think last night with all the others around was the right time to tell you."

A lightness filled Urskin, and he felt his breath catch in his throat. "I love you, too, Warsaw." Then he leaned forward and pressed his lips to Warsaw's in a light kiss. He kept the move chaste, putting space between them and relaxing back on the ground. Holding Warsaw's gaze, seeing the happy, contented streaks within his aura, Urskin sighed with his own contentment. "So, have you thought about what you wanted to do after you finished your restitution?"

"Uh, yeah."

Warsaw cast about, searching for something. He dragged what must have been the remains of his jeans to his side.

Urskin waited patiently as his shifter searched his pockets. He pulled out his phone, looking relieved when it turned on. "You're a bit of a nomad, right?" Warsaw asked as he swiped and tapped repeatedly at the device.

"I am," Urskin replied slowly. "But if I need to change that somewhat—"

When Warsaw swiftly shook his head, Urskin fell silent.

"Jasmine loves to go for rides." Warsaw held out his phone to Urskin. "I thought maybe we could travel together." He hesitated a second before adding, "I've never had a chance to see much of the country."

Urskin peered at the picture and smiled. A large motorcycle with a sidecar dominated the screen. In the sidecar, buckled into a harness, sat a very happy-looking Jasmine.

Meeting Warsaw's gaze, Urskin grinned. "Sounds like a plan."

Urskin would be more than happy to take his familiar anywhere he wanted to go.

Warsaw grinned back and hauled Urskin into a kiss that Urskin would gratefully accept . . . at every opportunity possible.

ABOUT THE AUTHOR

Charlie started writing fantasy when she was eight, and after stumbling onto her first erotic romance at age nineteen, she realized her true calling. She now focuses on writing gay erotic romance, normally of the paranormal variety, with heroes of all kinds. With the help and support of her husband, Charlie finally fulfilled one of her life-long goals . . . move to acreage with her horses. You can often find her curled up with her laptop and a cup of tea or glass of wine, creating her next adventure. Charlie enjoys exploring the mountains of her new Oregon home on horseback, 4-wheeler, or motorcycle.

She can be reached at ch.richards2010@yahoo.com
Or visit her at www.charlie-richards.com.

www.ingramcontent.com/pod-product-compliance
Lightning Source LLC
Chambersburg PA
CBHW070455130626
46555CB00003B/1010